Tom Titterly
The Novelist, 231 p + Index

Copyright 2020 Intermedia Educational Co. Ltd
ISBN 978-1-896574-05-9

Published, 2020, by Transmedia Translating and
Publishing Co., a branch of Intermedia Educational Co.
Ltd, 2701-2 Forest Laneway, Toronto, Ontario, M2N 5X7.
Phone:1-647-454-0220.
Email: intermediaeducational@gmail.com
Printed & distributed, Kindle Direct Publishing, Amazon.

Cover: Mark Ziaian

THE
NOVELIST

Tom Titterly

I would like to dedicate this book to Mark Ziaian without whom I would not have existed as a writer.

Table of Contents

Prologue

It was a warm Tuesday afternoon when Tom's life changed forever. A crowd had gathered at a bookshop for the book signing by a semi-famous author. With no interest at all in such matters, Tom decided to cross the road to avoid the end of the queue that had reached the pavement outside the bookshop. While crossing the road he was struck by a notion and by the time he had reached the other side of the road, he was determined to write a novel. He had a strong feeling that he had always wanted to be a novelist but could not remember why or when it had all begun, and moreover, had absolutely no idea what to write about. In the ensuing days, he asked his friends and family for ideas, but they couldn't really help him.

A few weeks later, Tom was sitting on a rock under the sun in his garden when his grandfather walked up to him and interrupted his thoughts.

"What's on your mind, son?"

Tom told his grandfather that he was looking for an idea for a novel.

"Do you remember when you were a child, I used to tell you stories? Well, all those stories were true. They were from my own experiences."

"But I don't have any interesting experiences," replied Tom.

"Well, why don't you go and meet people who do," advised his grandfather.

Tom thought that it would take a very long time to meet someone with an interesting story to tell, so he decided to speed things up by travelling, where he would hopefully come across people with tales to tell. He thought he should look into a trip around Europe, so while his mother was cooking lunch, he popped down to the local travel agency to ask what the best way was to see as much of the continent as possible. He returned with a plan, which he told his family about during lunch.

He was going to buy an Interrail ticket and travel all over Europe. The ticket would allow him to travel by train for a whole month.

His mother thought it was a fantastic idea and so did his younger brother George, who wished he could go with him.

"But what will you do for food?" his mother asked, passing him the basket of bread.

"Well, they do have food on the continent," Tom replied, "I'll just have to make sure I stick to a budget."

"What about accommodation?" his father inquired.

"I'll sleep mostly on night trains," Tom said confidently. "There are plenty of cheap hostels too. I can sleep anywhere, even on a park bench if I have to."

"You don't want to sleep on a park bench," his mother snapped. "You know what kind of people sleep there."

"People like Tom", said George, looking a bit smug for coming up with what he must have thought was a witty answer.

"Oh, I hope you don't meet some girl over there and leave us to spend the rest of your life abroad," his mother said with a tone that was difficult to tell whether she was joking or genuinely worried.

"I spent all those years away from you at uni and didn't meet the girl of my dreams; I hardly think I'm going to meet and marry a girl on my first trip abroad," Tom said reassuringly.

"If he does marry and move abroad, we'll have somewhere to spend our holidays," said George, lighting up the conversation.

"He'll be fine," his grandfather said. "He's a bright young man who knows what he wants to do and seems to have all angles covered. He'll probably learn more about real life in one month than he did in all those years at university."

His grandmother, who had been mostly silent, chewing a challenging piece of meat, nodded to agree with her husband.

A few days later, Tom bought the ticket to start his journey the following Monday and began to pack his haversack and say goodbye to his envious friends. Tom was still a university student, though he had taken a year off and moved back with his parents, taking temporary jobs to make some money and prepare himself for his final year. He had been hoping to find another job in the summer, but now he had put everything on hold to explore Europe.

Day 1 Monday

It was early Monday morning, when having just seen his father set off to work, Tom kissed his mother and hugged his brother George goodbye and walked down to the bus stop with a feeling of great excitement tinged with slight nervousness at what lay ahead. The bus became visible in the distance and when he got on, he felt that he was moving into unknown territory even though he had been on that bus many times before. It was a warm sunny day, just as you would expect for early July. He looked out of the bus window, watching people going about their daily lives, knowing that on that particular day he was different. He was leaving them all behind. Soon enough the bus reached its destination where he took a local train to the main railway station. He asked a guard from which platform the train would be leaving and stood at the platform waiting for the train to arrive.

When the train was over ten minutes late, Tom began to worry and asked another guard how long the train would be. He was informed that the train had left on time and that the first guard had misinformed him about the number of the platform. He would now have to wait three more hours for the next train. He made sure of the correct platform and began his long wait. An hour later he heard a familiar voice. It was his mother who had arrived with sandwiches for him, somehow knowing that he had probably missed his train. When he did get on the train his long wait had given him a sense of relief rather than excitement. He took his seat and was soon on his way.

Quite a few of the passengers were also young backpackers, but it was only when he got on the ferry and saw the white cliffs of Dover fading into the distance that he felt like a real traveller. He began to explore the ferry avoiding the temptation to spend money, as he knew it had to last him a whole month. He decided to go up on deck for some fresh air and sunshine and his first photos of the trip. He asked a young girl who was reading a book if she wouldn't mind taking his picture. She seemed friendly, and after she had taken a few pictures, Tom introduced himself and asked the girl, who sounded foreign, if she had enjoyed her time in the U.K.

The young girl, Claudia, said that she was German and had been visiting a friend who was working in England. It transpired that she had gone over to work as a nanny.

"I saw advertised in a German newspaper that a couple were looking for a nanny to take care of their three-year-olds Russel and Jack. I thought looking after three-year-old twin boys would be a good challenge for me and I would learn better English, but when I arrived, I noticed that they had a small dog and no children. I think the newspaper had made a bad translation. The man of the house was Adrian who said that he worked in the market, but he always wore a suit to work and carried a briefcase, so I don't think he sold fruit. I think he was a financial man. His wife was called Luda and was from Eastern Europe, so her English was not perfect, but that didn't matter because she never had conversations with me. She just used to order me around and if she couldn't find anything for me to do, she would send me out to buy her cigarettes or take the dog for a walk. But Adrian was friendly and would treat me normally and talk to me until Luda would stop him and take him away by telling him not to fraternise with the staff. At least I learnt one word from her. I felt very uncomfortable in her company.

"One day she sent me out with the dog to buy cigarettes and said that I could buy myself some chocolate too. I was away for about 45 minutes and walked straight in when I got back as the front door was open. I thought perhaps she was going to do something in the front garden but when I walked into the kitchen, I saw that she was tied up to a chair. She said that a man had forced his way in and robbed them. She said that he had taken all her jewellery, her cash and credit cards and many other valuable items from the house. It wasn't long before her husband arrived and phoned the police. They said that he must have been a professional thief with a lot of experience as he had been able to break into Adrian's safe where he kept a large amount of cash for emergencies. About a week later Adrian and Luda were going to a dinner party. I didn't want to be left alone after what had just happened, but Adrian said that he would put the burglar alarm on and instructed me not to open the door to anyone. It was then that I noticed Luda was wearing a pair of earrings that had been reported stolen. When I mentioned it to her, she shouted at me and said that they had been her favourite earrings, so she had bought an identical pair days after the robbery. I remember admiring them while I was dusting her dressing table the first week I was there and as I paid close attention under the sunlight; I noticed a very small stone missing from one of them. When I pointed this out Adrian demanded to inspect the earrings and under close inspection found that, as I had said, there was a very small stone missing. After several minutes of interrogation by Adrian, Luda broke down and admitted that she had met a man who had planned the robbery with her. Adrian was very angry and shouted at her so much that his face became red and Luda left in tears with Adrian shouting that he never wanted to see her again without a divorce lawyer.

After Luda left, Adrian poured himself a glass of whiskey and when he had calmed down, he phoned his hosts and said that his wife had gone down with food poisoning and they couldn't make it. I was quite shaken but started to go over everything in my mind. I should have known that she was involved when she told me that the thief had taken all her jewellery. She couldn't have known what he had taken from the bedroom when she was tied up in the kitchen and a thief would want everything to look normal from outside so he would have closed the front door. Unless he wanted her to be discovered quickly. I should have known that she must have been the one to give him the combination to the safe. I felt quite stupid for not noticing these things straight away. By that time Adrian had drunk several glasses of whiskey and after cursing his wife, he began to tell me how beautiful and efficient I was and how he admired these qualities in a young woman. He told me that he had a surprise for me and staggered upstairs to return after a few minutes dressed in women's underwear with a dead flower between his teeth. This was not the kind of surprise I was expecting, and as he made his intention towards me clearer, I felt more and more uncomfortable and vulnerable. Luckily, he was more playful than violent, so I managed to get away from him and lock myself in my room where I packed my bag and took the first opportunity to get out of the house.

"I knew that I couldn't change the date on my flight ticket because I had looked into it after only one week when I wasn't getting on well with Luda, and in fact I didn't really want to go back to Koblenz without any good experiences from England, so I decided to visit a German friend who was living in Leeds. I didn't have her phone number, but she had recently celebrated a birthday and I had sent her a card, so I had her address. It was the early hours of the morning when I rang her doorbell. She was sleepy but happy to see me and made me feel very welcome. I had a great two weeks with her and during this time found out that both Luda and Adrian had been arrested for trying to cheat the insurance company. I understand that they had taken their valuable things to another place one or two days before the fake robbery. Luda had opened the front door and tied herself up to use me as a witness. I remember after taking the tape off her mouth I was going to untie her, but she shouted at me and told me to cut her free with a sharp knife. Probably she didn't want me to discover how easily she could have been untied. I think they had planned that Luda would take the blame if I became suspicious so that the responsibility of informing the police would fall to Adrian and not me. Adrian's final act was to make me leave without him breaking our work contract. He hadn't actually touched me, so I wasn't going to report him, but he did enough for me to know that I couldn't work there anymore. I believe as soon as I left, Luda was back with Adrian and so were all their belongings. The police discovered what they had done a week later when they caught a real thief leaving the house with many of their things that had already been reported stolen."

"I hope this hasn't put you off England," Tom enquired with a tinge of concern in his voice.

"Not at all," Claudia smiled reassuringly. "I would like to see more of England, and I still have my return flight ticket left, so I will come back to England by train or coach two or three weeks before that date and fly back to Germany so that my ticket isn't wasted."

By the time Tom and Claudia reached France they had become friends and exchanged addresses. Tom said that she could spend some time with him next time she visits

England and as he continued to travel down to Paris by train her voice echoed in his head and he began to miss her company.

It felt strange to hear everyone speaking French and it took Tom a bit of getting used to as he had never been abroad before. When he arrived in Paris it was a nice sunny day and he started to look for a hotel, but they all seemed to be above his price range. In one of the hotels, he met Brian, an Englishman who had also gone in looking for a reasonably priced hotel. Brian told him that he had been looking for several hours and had come to the conclusion that he would have to venture to the outskirts of Paris to find cheaper accommodation. Tom didn't want to give up Paris and tried some youth hostels, but they were all full up. Finally, he decided to go back to the station and take a train to a place with fewer tourists and find cheaper accommodation.

About half an hour later, the train stopped at a small station that appealed to him, and he decided to try his luck as it was beginning to get late and he needed to find a place to sleep. He got off the train and stood on the only platform and as the train disappeared from his view he started to walk towards the street when a man said something to him in French. Tom didn't speak French and told the man that he was from England. The Frenchman didn't speak English but understood where Tom was from and said, "Liverpool." Tom smiled and said, "Paris Saint Germain." The little man's round face lit up and asked a question, which Tom didn't fully understand but uttered the word "hotel". The man said, "No, no, no" and pointed to his wedding ring saying, "Liverpool". He beckoned Tom to follow him, taking him to a taxi that was parked outside the station. Tom tried to make it clear that he didn't want a taxi, but the man put the palms of his hands over the

9

meter and moved them towards and away from each other to assure him that the ride would be free. After a short drive, the taxi stopped outside a small block of flats. The taxi driver seemed quite popular in the village as quite a few of the shopkeepers who were sitting outside their shops had greeted him as he had driven past. The taxi driver asked Tom to follow him as he got out of the parked taxi and entered a building. He went up to the second floor, opened the door and said something in French. Tom was greeted by a little fat lady who in broken English said that she was the taxi driver's wife and had once been to Liverpool. She told Tom that he could stay there for a few days and showed him to a room with a bed and several bookcases with quite a lot of books. Tom put his things down and thanked the couple, using one of the few words he knew in French.

The sun was setting, and Tom thought it would be nice to go for a walk to see a bit more of the village, so he moved two fingers in a walking gesture pointing with his nose to the front door. The couple said, "Oui, oui" and something else that Tom didn't understand.

The fresh evening air and the calm reminded Tom that he was on holiday as he walked through the streets just following his nose enjoying being far away from his usual life. He thought about his family and friends and imagined that they would be doing the usual things back home. After about half an hour he decided to walk back to the taxi driver's flat where he would be spending the night. He turned around and began his journey back, but soon realised that he was not sure how to find his way. Suddenly he felt the darkness even more and began to panic slightly, remembering that he had left his belongings including his passport at a place that he was unsure he could find. After walking around for about ten minutes, hoping to see a street or building he recognised, he noticed a young lady on a balcony combing her hair and tried to draw her attention for help. She seemed confused and shouted a few words in French. A vicious-looking man wearing a string vest appeared behind her and started to shout at Tom. Tom asked if he spoke English.

The man said, "No!"

Tom said, "Taxi" and mimed a little man with a moustache.

The man suddenly calmed down and smiled, pointing directions and showing numbers with his fingers. Tom felt a sense of relief knowing that he was not completely lost. He was happy to see the taxi driver and his wife when he finally found their flat after the near scare.

By that time their son, who could speak English, had joined them. The talkative Frenchman talked for what seemed like forever about British politics and music.

Tom was very tired after a long day, and it showed. He was glad that he had a genuine excuse to be excused. This was the first time that Tom was sleeping abroad, and he slept like a log.

Day 2 Tuesday

The next day Tom awoke quite early to the sound of the French language and thought that the taxi driver would probably want to be working during the morning rush hour, so he rose quickly and after a hurried breakfast was driven to the station and told that he would be picked up at six p.m. Tom was a considerate young man and had rushed to get ready so as not to keep the taxi driver from work. He needn't have worried; the taxi driver had to sit in his taxi for more than 15 minutes before the first train arrived, and no one got off.

Tom took the next train to Paris where he started to look for the Eiffel Tower, which was not difficult to find. Most people knew what Tom was looking for and pointed him in the right direction almost before he had finished his question. One of the people he asked was a young girl who answered in an American accent. Rebecca was an American who had been living in Paris for six months where she was working as a secretary and learning French. She accompanied him to the Eiffel Tower. It was another warm sunny day and the many tourists snapping away at their cameras reminded him that he had left that morning without his camera.

Tom and Rebecca spent some hours together and seemed to get along well. Rebecca invited Tom into her flat where she picked up a book that she had to return to a friend later that evening. Tom noticed that there were a lot of miniature elephants in the flat but decided not to question her taste and hoped that the reason for her collection would come out in conversation or become clear as he got to know her better. Rebecca said that she had to go to work and asked if he would like to meet her the next day. As they walked towards her metro station, they agreed to meet the following day at three o'clock under the Eiffel Tower.

Just as Rebecca disappeared through the ticket barrier, Tom turned and came face to face with two girls who had heard him speaking English and were wondering if he could recommend a cheap hotel. Tom said that he was staying with a taxi driver he had met and shared the little knowledge he had of Paris hotels with the two girls who introduced themselves as Debbie and Tracy. They both agreed that the hotels Tom had seen were too expensive and with the help of their map, a bit of guesswork and quite a lot of legwork found themselves in an area less desirable than central Paris where everything seemed to be more abundant and affordable. The girls felt more secure and confident in the company of Tom who himself was interested in finding a cheap hotel for future reference.

"I won an art competition back home in California," Tracy said with a hint of pride. "The prize was a round-trip ticket to Paris for me and a friend with some cash thrown in, but to claim the prize I had to agree to find a hotel myself and paint some pictures to capture the ambience of the surrounding areas. I chose my best friend Debbie as my travel companion. We are planning to take lots of photographs during our one-week stay, and I will also draw some sketches to work from when I get back. It will save me from having to fly with paintings that could get damaged in the flight and would probably cost a lot to check in."

Tracy was enthusiastically looking forward to her time in Paris, saying that she wanted to hit as many art galleries and museums as possible. On the other hand, all Debbie did was complain. She said that the flight was too long with inflight food that was ready-made and probably out of a tin and that Paris was not what she had expected.

"Why do we have to find a cheap hotel?" Debbie complained. "They gave us a lot of spending money."

"We are not planning to spend much time in the hotel room, so I think it would be wiser to use the money on better food and entertainment rather than waste it on an expensive hotel in the center of Paris that would probably be noisy at night because of the heavy traffic," Tracy explained.

Debbie and Tracy seemed happy with the third hotel they walked into and decided to stay there, leaving Tom without a thank you or goodbye as they attended to the formalities at the desk before walking up the narrow stairs to their room. A few moments later Tom heard Debbie yell "Oh my God. Have you seen the bathroom? It's awful." Tom knew from the short time he had spent with the girls how much Debbie enjoyed complaining and expected her to express her negative views about the room, just not so loudly and with so much revulsion. He chuckled as he walked away from the hotel feeling a bit sorry for Tracy.

Walking the streets of Paris aimlessly, soaking up the atmosphere and observing Parisian life on his first full day abroad was so engrossing that he almost forgot he had a train to catch and without a map had no idea how to get to the station. He asked for directions to the train station and having remembered the number from the previous day walked straight to the platform, but everything was different and after a moment of confusion it dawned on him that there was more than one station in Paris and he was at the wrong one. Luckily the station he wanted wasn't far away and he managed to jump onto the train just as it was about to depart. The girls had shared some of their food with Tom as they had sat down on a bench on their way to the hotel, but with so much walking he was beginning to feel peckish and quite thirsty too.

Tom returned to the village regretting not writing down the taxi driver's address and wondering how he would find the flat if he needed to, but to his relief, the taxi driver was waiting outside the station to take him back to his flat.

That evening the taxi driver's wife had prepared a special meal, and they were joined once again by their son Pierre, who seemed more relaxed than the previous night when he had unleashed his limited knowledge of the English language upon the poor unsuspecting Tom. This time he asked Tom how he had enjoyed Paris and listened to his answer with interest before sitting down to concentrate on the many varieties of seafood he so enjoyed. Seafood was not Tom's cup of tea but luckily there was plenty of fish that Tom was more accustomed to. There was also plenty to drink. After a long day in Paris, the cold beer went down a treat. Tom couldn't wait to see what they had to offer for dessert and was initially disappointed when a tray of cheeses arrived, but he soon began to join in and enjoy the full selection. After the meal, Mrs taxi driver brought a photo album to show Tom. The taxi driver explained who the people in the photographs were and Pierre translated. Tom recognised that some of the pictures had been taken in England.

"These pictures were taken in Liverpool," Pierre said excitedly. "My mother went to a concert in Liverpool many years ago when she was a young girl. After the concert, she noticed that her moneybag containing her passport and return ticket had disappeared. She was travelling with two friends who had very little English between them and had resigned herself to the idea of having to hitchhike to the French embassy in London for help. Her friends told her that the local police might help her with a train ticket to London. When she asked at the police station, a police officer who spoke a little French with a strong English accent asked her to wait, and when he returned moments later, he handed her an envelope. To her surprise and delight, inside the envelope was her moneybag containing everything she thought she had lost. Now thanks to the kindness and honesty of the person who handed in her belongings, my mother has a soft spot for the English. And my father is also fond of the English as he is a huge fan of Nottingham Forest."

Pierre left just before midnight, saying that he had to go to work the next morning. With Pierre gone, Tom finished his drink, said goodnight and ended his first full day abroad in a cosy bed surrounded by books.

Day 3 Wednesday

The next day after breakfast, Tom gathered his belongings, thanked Mrs taxi driver and was driven to the station where he took the train to Paris. It was still early, and many Parisians were rushing to work. Tom had a lot of time to spend before meeting Rebecca and was sure she could show him the main sights which he would enjoy even more in her company, so he decided to follow his nose and walk around trying to avoid familiar places and venture into new territories. He sauntered around the streets of Paris spending a lot of time watching street entertainers and walking into shops to see the local fashion while absorbing the ambience of Paris in the process. By one o'clock, all the walking had made him hungry, so he bought a large baguette and juice and found a nearby park where he sat on a bench to rejuvenate. As he ripped part of the baguette off into a manageable size, his action was witnessed by a girl who was passing his bench. She stopped and asked him in English where he had bought his food. Tom gave her directions to the shop that was not far from the park. She was wearing brown trousers and a green top that reminded Tom of a tree, and she had an accent that he did not recognize, but knew it was not French.

Tom was ready to leave when the girl dressed in the colours of a tree returned from the shop with a few paper bags in her hands, and as the nearby benches were all partially occupied, gravitated towards Tom's bench where he welcomed her by moving away from the centre of the bench to make room for her. Tom had finished eating but tore a piece off the remainder of his baguette and continued eating to keep the girl company as she began to eat what

17

she had bought from the shop. He noticed that she didn't have any luggage with her and assumed that she had left it in a locker at the railway station.

"Have you left your luggage in a locker?" Tom asked.

"No, I'm staying with a friend," she replied. "There's plenty of food in her fridge, but I forgot the spare key she gave me and can't get in until she gets back from work after five o'clock. It's her last day at work before her holidays. Tomorrow we are going to Hungary, so I really should be eating food from her fridge before it goes off. I'm Gudrun from Iceland. The girl I'm staying with was staying at the hotel in Iceland where I was working as a receptionist last summer. We became friends when we discovered that we both knew sign language, played the piano and enjoyed reading the same books. I said that she could stay with me to save money on the hotel. Now I am staying with her."

Tom introduced himself and said that he had never met anyone from Iceland before.

"How come you know sign language?"

"A long time ago, a young Icelandic man called Ragnar was on a train in Denmark when he noticed a girl joyfully communicating with some children in sign language. He had learnt this language and was keen to practice but even keener to get to know the girl, so he drew her attention and they signed across the train. Before reaching his stop, he asked if he could see her again. She said that she was having a few friends over the following evening and asked him to arrive early. The next evening as he approached her flat, he wondered what it would be like to date a deaf girl but all he could see was her smile. When he got out of the lift, she was waiting for him at the front door. She showed him to the living room where he sat for a few minutes while she finished preparing food in the kitchen. Shortly after joining him in the living room, the phone rang and to his amazement, she answered it. Not only could she talk, but she could speak Icelandic. The person on the phone was a friend who said that she couldn't make it that evening and as she was also driving the other two guests asked if she didn't mind meeting some other evening instead. Ragnar and the girl didn't mind at all, as they had plenty to talk about. Two years later they moved back to Iceland, married and had a daughter they called Gudrun, who is sitting on this bench right now. My parents taught both me and my younger sister sign language as it was the language that brought them together. My father was very handsome when he was young. I wouldn't be surprised if my mother asked her friend to phone and say that she couldn't come, so that she could be alone with him."

Tom and Gudrun, who had been walking around in the park, continued talking and forgot about the time until Tom noticed that it was almost three o'clock and he was going to meet Rebecca at that time. He exchanged addresses with Gudrun and told her that he had to rush to the station to catch a train, though he immediately felt guilty about lying to her. He walked rapidly towards the Eiffel Tower with his quick steps turning to the occasional run, but when he reached their agreed meeting point it was already ten minutes past three and Rebecca was nowhere to be seen. He felt deflated and blamed himself for not being on time, but then began to blame Rebecca for not waiting. After more than half an hour, Tom was just about to leave when he spotted Rebecca walking towards him among the crowd. She was wearing a red t-shirt, which he found particularly attractive with her blond hair.

"I'm sorry I'm late," she said. "I just couldn't get away from work as early as I had hoped. Though I shouldn't complain. Most people have to stay and work until five."

Tom concurred that it was nice to have a flexible job and asked her how she had ended up in Paris. Rebecca, who liked to be called Becky, said that she had always liked the French language and lifestyle.

"I suppose you could say that I'm a Francophile. I had taken a sabbatical and treated myself to a trip to Paris. On my third day, I found a wallet outside a cafe and discovered that it belonged to a fellow American called Donald Steele whom I traced with the help of the American embassy. The wallet-loser was so impressed with my honesty and the initiative I had shown to find him, that when he learned of my desire to spend more time in France, made a phone call and arranged a job interview which by the nature of it seemed like a formality. It was almost as if the job was already in the bag. I never saw Donald again despite several attempts to find him. Nobody at my workplace had ever heard of him and even my boss denied knowing such a person. The embassy said that they could not give out personal information. The mystery baffled me, especially when the French immigration office said that no such person had ever existed on their records."

Tom had grown fond of Becky, but as they walked around the sights and parks of Paris where they watched a few games of pétanque played by elderly Parisian gentlemen and enjoyed the architecture on their way to the railway station, he knew that he would not be seeing her for a while. It was his last day in Paris and soon he would be on his way to Belgium.

As the train pulled out of the station and the waving Becky disappeared into the distance all he could think of was the long passionate goodbye kiss he had regretfully been too shy to initiate. He was sure that it was what Becky had wanted, but not sure enough.

Tom had just made himself comfortable in his seat when a mother and daughter took their places opposite him and Tom helped put their luggage on the overhead rack.

They were Belgian and had been shopping in Paris. The mother seemed to like Tom and the way she was talking about her daughter Marion, felt a bit like matchmaking. Tom and Marion felt a bit uncomfortable, so they took over the conversation. Perhaps that was the idea. Marion's long brown curly hair and innocent smile was somewhat overshadowed by her long shapely legs and her tight shorts that left very little to the imagination.

By the time they reached Liege, Tom and Marion had enjoyed each other's company, and the mother seemed to be happy for her daughter.

"I can help you find a youth hostel if you don't mind us taking our shopping home and having a coffee first," Marion said.

The mother's car was parked at the station, and she drove them to their home on the outskirts of Liege. As the mother got out of the car and approached her front door her rummaging in her handbag became more and more intense until she suddenly stopped and said, "Oh my God, I have forgotten my front-door keys. How are we going to get in?" They noticed a small window was slightly open. The women looked at Tom and then at the small window. It wouldn't be easy to climb up and squeeze through, but Tom said that he would give it a go. A few minutes later Tom was on the other side of the front door letting the hosts in. They were both grateful to have such a "hero" there to save the day. After they had sat down for coffee and biscuits Tom was ready to be taken to the local youth hostel, but the mother suggested that he could spend the night at their place.

Tom was getting ready to go out for a walk with Marion when a balding man walked in, extended his hand and introduced himself as Marion's father Marcel. Soon the table was set and they all sat for supper. The hosts consciously made an effort to speak English and seemed to enjoy it. Marcel said that he was in marketing and had played competitive chess for many years. He mentioned several British chess players he had faced, but of course, Tom had never heard of any of them. After supper, Marion said that she had a headache and was very tired after her shopping spree in Paris. She retired leaving Tom and her father to chat while her mother put the dishes in the dishwasher and continued doing things in the kitchen. The two men moved to the living room with some beer and two glasses in Marcel's hands.

"You must have travelled a lot because of chess. Have you got any interesting stories to tell?" asked Tom.

"Yes," replied Marcel, "probably the most amazing thing that happened to me was when I was in Tashkent. My Uzbek opponent completely overlooked my bishop and I beat him after only 4 minutes and 24 seconds." Tom regretted his question, but Marcel continued, "With the match finishing about an hour earlier than I had expected, I decided to take a relaxing stroll back to my hotel. I was halfway there when dark clouds gathered and suddenly the heaviest rain I have even seen started to pour from the heavens. I had nowhere to shelter so I began to run blindly. I had only run about 30 meters when a car stopped beside me and a door opened. I instinctively got into the car and thanked the driver, commenting on the atrocious weather. The driver continued to drive without a word, and I soon realised that he had no intention of dropping me off at my hotel. I repeated the name of the hotel several times, and as I got louder the driver drove faster. I don't remember what happened next, but I do remember waking up and seeing before me the most beautiful girl I had ever seen. As she began to speak Flemish in a soft gentle voice, I remember thinking that I had died and gone to heaven. She told me that her name was Helen and that she had been there on a medical mission and was about to return to Belgium when it had become known that a Belgian national had been involved in a car accident, so she had been asked to stay a bit longer. I had been the victim of a kidnapping. The kidnappers had put a lot of money on my final opponent to win the tournament and wanted to make sure I didn't get in his way. I'm not sure whether they wanted to try and persuade me to throw the match or just keep me away until after the final, but after the failed kidnapping their plot was revealed, and their bets were annulled. Luckily, I recovered from the car crash and was released from hospital within a few days in time to play in the final. They needn't have bothered kidnapping me as I lost the final, but I am glad they did, otherwise, I probably would never have met my lovely wife, Helen."

When Helen had finished doing what she was doing in the kitchen, she looked at Marcel and said goodnight to Tom on her way to the bathroom. Both men understood that it was time to sleep and though Marcel told Tom that he could help himself to more beer and watch television if he was not tired, but Tom decided to call it a day.

Day 4 Thursday

When Tom woke up the next day, the house was quiet. He had heard people leaving for work earlier but had decided to continue sleeping. He put on his clothes and went into the living room, where Marion was sitting reading the daily paper. He was glad to hear that her headache was better and that she had recovered physically from her long day in Paris.

"You can take a shower before breakfast if you want," Marion said. "The green towel is for you to use."

When Tom emerged from the bathroom, the smell of fresh coffee was even stronger than before and there was bread, a variety of jams and several cartons of cereal on the kitchen table.

"I've already had my first cup of coffee," Marion said, "Do you take yours with milk and sugar?"

"Just milk, please!" Thinking that he would have preferred tea had he been given the choice.

"I have to go to work in the afternoon, but we could hang out until then if you want," Marion suggested. "Is there anything special you'd like to do or see?"

"No, not really. It's my first time in Belgium, so everything will be new and interesting for me. I'd like to see the places that mean something to you, before I catch my train to the Netherlands later today."

Not long after breakfast, Tom took his haversack, Marion her shoulder bag and they left the house. They walked leisurely along the river.

"I like walking here," she said. "A few months ago, I met a foul-mouthed but loveable Dutchman called Ernie. I had never met anyone like him. He would give money to homeless people while verbally abusing them. I never saw him without a beer in his hand, but he was never drunk, and he smoked like a chain but only every other week. He said that he liked smoking but wanted to prove to himself that he was not addicted and could give it up at any time. Ernie lived a simple life and wasn't interested in money, though he was never without cash. When I met him, he was living rent-free in a boat that belonged to a friend of his. He did interior decorating from time to time and used something he called feng shui without charging anything. People liked him and would usually insist on paying or doing him favours. I used to hang out with him a lot because I found his philosophy of life and the people he mixed with interesting. He taught me to be more confident in myself and through him I met some very good artists and successful people.

"About ten days ago he suddenly told me that he had found a very cheap ticket to the Philippines and would be leaving straight away. He said that he wanted to travel around Asia to discover his spirituality and told me that he would send me his thoughts if I walked along the river and concentrated. I soon began to hear rumours that he had become a father in the Philippines and that is why he had travelled there. I was very disappointed because I thought he was an open and honest person and expected him to tell me the truth. He had had a lot of casual relationships and had a reputation for it, but he always treated me like a sister, even though my mother didn't believe me and thought that I was heartbroken when he left. This is why she planned the trip to Paris and tried to do some matchmaking between you and me. She wanted to take my mind off him, but by that time I had already heard from him. He said that he had been in a relationship with a girl in his hometown several years ago. When the girl returned to her native Philippines, she found out that she was pregnant but was unable to contact him as he didn't have a fixed address. He said that it was by chance that he had found the cheap ticket and was on a mission to discover his spirituality but somehow felt the urge to go and look her up when he got there. The three-year-old boy had been asking questions about his father and one day had cried himself to sleep. The next day Ernie arrived at their doorstep. As a single mother, she was living with her parents who were still living at the same address she had given Ernie. He said that he sensed such a strong connection with his son that he no longer needed to search for his spirituality and had decided to settle down."

Tom felt he had known Marion for a long time. They had travelled from Paris together and he even knew her family history. He liked the family and felt sure that they would meet again. Marion showed Tom the local bowling alley where she was working. They had a few games and some spaghetti before going to the station where Tom asked Marion to thank her parents for their hospitality and gave her his contact details.

On the train, Tom looked at his map and remembered Claudia when he saw Koblenz to the east of Liege. But he was on his way to Rotterdam and was soon standing on the platform at the station. He needed a cheap place to stay, so he started to look around for signs and saw the information centre. They gave him a list of hotels and a map, but as he exited armed with his new information, he heard an American accent and turned around to see a young man with goggle eyes who told him that he had stayed at a place that was dead cheap but decent if he didn't mind sleeping on a mattress on the floor. He gave Tom a piece of paper with an address and a hand-drawn map as if he was bequeathing him a treasure. Tom thanked him and headed off in the direction that the American had given him. Tom registered at the place, and yes it did look cheap. There was a room with some mattresses on the floor and some up against the wall for future use. The manager told Tom that he could choose a mattress and reserve it by putting his sleeping bag on it if he wanted to go out.

Having left his haversack inside his sleeping bag in the poor disguise of a small sleeping person or possibly to make it more difficult to pilfer, Tom hit the town walking for hours like a true tourist watching Rotterdam's evening and then nightlife unfold. English could be heard a lot more than in the other cities Tom had visited so far and with the hand-drawn map in his back pocket, he felt more confident in finding his way back to the hostel when the time was right. The pubs and restaurants were becoming more and more tempting until he failed to pass a kebab shop and found himself ordering an extra spicy kebab which was within his budget. Having been walking for several hours, Tom decided to enjoy his kebab in a seated position. There were several pictures on the wall that were unmistakably from Turkey, but one was completely different and stood out from the rest.

"My world came crashing down when I lost a pair of gloves I had recently bought", Tom heard while his gaze was still fixated on the odd picture. The man who was sitting on the stool next to Tom's seemed friendly and sober despite his strange opening line. He was quite smartly dressed and as Tom acknowledged his presence, he continued to talk. "I'm from Switzerland where I was living with my wife in a small rented flat, saving up to buy a property. I got the gloves in the sale for an exceptionally good price. I felt very lucky as they were the last ones in the shop and exactly what I had wanted. They had fallen behind some other items and that is probably why no one

27

had picked them up. I felt that they were meant for me. A few days later I had an important meeting with a client who was flying in and I was going to meet him at his hotel. I wore my lucky gloves for the first time and that gave me extra confidence. My wife was going to have her hair done at a new hairdresser's later that day, so she was happy too. I went to the office and did some paperwork in my final preparation for the meeting that was going to be over lunch at my client's hotel. I arrived at the hotel early and went straight to the hotel's restaurant to order a cup of coffee. It was cold outside, and I felt that I needed a coffee before meeting my client. I hadn't been there long when I heard my name being called. Expecting to see my client I turned around, but it was someone from the front desk who informed me that my client had called to say that there had been a mix-up and that he was staying at another hotel across town. I quickly finished off my coffee, paid for it and left in a hurry. I hadn't gone far when I noticed that one of my gloves was missing. I rushed back to the hotel and as I entered, I saw an attractive woman with my glove in her hand walking towards me. When she saw me, she smiled, raised her hand slightly and said, "I think this belongs to you". I thanked her as we left the hotel. She told me that she saw it on the floor when she was putting on her coat and would have handed it in at the reception but thought that it would save me a lot of time and bother if she could catch up with me and give it to me herself. Once again, I thanked her for her quick thinking and kindness as I set off to the hotel where my client was staying, feeling good about life. The meeting went very well, and I secured an excellent deal for the company, which I was sure would give me a bonus and maybe even a promotion. I returned home that day with a smile on my face and told my wife about my success. She asked me what my client's name was, what he looked like and where we had met, but showed very little interest in my answers and blanked out completely when I started to talk about the business side of things. I suddenly realised that I had committed the sin of not complimenting her on her new hairstyle. I told her how pretty her hair looked, but that just seemed to make things worse. She became cold and distant. Several months passed and our relationship did not improve. I couldn't believe that she was unwilling to forgive me for not mentioning her hair ahead of my success. She had been rejecting my occasional romantic gestures, but it still came to me as a shock when she announced that she wanted a divorce. She told me that she had met another man and that she had just found out that she was expecting his child. She said that she had seen me walk out of a hotel with a young woman at the same time that I had claimed to be on the other side of town conducting a business meeting and that her affair was meant to be a short-lived act of tit for tat. I was speechless. And during my speechlessness, I quickly decided not to defend myself. I saw no point in trying to save our marriage as she was carrying another man's child. I was furious. I packed a small bag and left. Ironically, I spent the night at the hotel where I had almost lost my glove. You could say, it was my love I lost not my glove. I could have stayed with a friend but wanted to be alone and think things over. That night I decided to make a fresh start in life. Within a week I had quit my job and was on a train to the Netherlands where my best friend lived. I had transferred all my money to his account so that my wife couldn't get her hands on it in the divorce. You might think I was cruel, but as it happened her lover turned out to be a conman and almost left her penniless. Luckily her pregnancy turned out to be a false alarm, probably brought on by the stress of thinking I was having an affair. On the train to the Netherlands, while passing through Germany, a Turkish man with a lot of luggage moved into my compartment. His name was Murat, and he was leaving his wife for a completely different reason. He had been promised a cleaning job in a hotel in Rotterdam and was planning to work as much as he physically could, to send money for his wife and children to have a better life. He said that his dream was to one day own a kebab shop back home. When we arrived, he moved in temporarily with a friend and his family in Rotterdam and I stayed with my friend who lives just outside the city. We kept in touch and after a while, knowing how passionate he was about the kebab business and as he had learnt to speak Dutch quite well, I suggested that I could invest my money in a kebab shop. He does all the work and keeps most of the profit while I do nothing and keep a percentage of the profit as the owner of the shop. His wife and children have now joined him in Rotterdam and seem to be very happy here, but he is still planning to go back to Turkey and buy his own shop when he has enough money. I married a wonderful Dutch girl and we have a 2-year-old son, but my ex-wife who cheated on me is still living alone. The picture you were looking at is of my lucky gloves. I still think they brought me luck because they showed me the true colours of the person whom I had been married to for almost two years and thought I knew. These gloves changed my destiny in life. I am extremely happy here, so I keep a picture of them in the shop to remind me where I came from and to bring me luck. We serve delicious food, but I think a strange picture of a pair of gloves on the wall makes the shop even more memorable."

When Tom returned to the hostel, he felt his way in the dark to where his mattress was, but his haversack was gone and instead, a bearded man was sleeping there. As he began to entertain thoughts of losing his belongings, his eyes became more accustomed to the dark and he noticed his sleeping bag bulging with what was surely his haversack in the far corner of the room next to a vacant mattress that was standing against the wall. He was soon lying in his sleeping bag on the mattress where he slept soundly until early the next morning.

Day 5 Friday

Tom decided to leave straight away so that he could see as much of Rotterdam in daylight as possible. Unfortunately, the hostel was still dark with all the curtains drawn and he tripped while going down the stairs. In an attempt to regain his balance, he instinctively reached out to hold onto the wooden bannister and got a huge splinter under the nail of his left ring finger. He spent the next half hour asking the way to the hospital where he was given a tetanus shot, had the splinter removed and his finger bandaged.

He had not yet had breakfast, so he bought a doughnut and some milk and found a bench where he sat down for breakfast while watching life go by the Dutch way. A woman was pushing a baby in a buggy with another small child by her side on a trike while an elderly woman was jogging by. Opposite him, a man and woman were sitting on a bench. The man appeared to have fallen asleep while reading a newspaper, but Tom noticed that he was about to open the young woman's handbag. The man's fingers slipped into the handbag when Tom leapt to his feet and released a mighty yell. In a split second the man dropped his newspaper and ran like a bat out of hell. The young woman, who had been unaware of what was unfolding, suddenly realised that she had been at the centre of an unpleasant incident and quickly began to search her bag to ensure that nothing was missing. Tom went over to make sure she was OK. She started to thank Tom in Dutch and quickly switched to English when she realised that Tom didn't speak any Dutch. She then burst into tears and Tom spent the next ten minutes comforting her until his reassuring words and sense of humour turned her tears into laughter.

"My name is Ellen by the way," said the tall Dutch girl who was almost as tall as Tom who himself stood at 182 cm.

Tom thought they should go to the police station and report the crime. He suggested that they should take the newspaper for fingerprints, but Ellen was more sceptical and said that she would rather put the whole thing behind her. She said that she had to return some books and asked if he would like to accompany her to the library. They talked about his trip and her studies among other things and after the library continued until they reached the university where she was studying. Tom could not believe how many bicycles there were. That was when a cyclist stopped beside them and very tall gangly man started to talk. Ellen introduced him as Dirk who was studying engineering and whom she knew from a photography club she had joined. Dirk welcomed Tom to Rotterdam and asked him what he had seen of the city.

"I think it is important to find out as much as possible about the place you are visiting. This university, for example, was founded in 1913. Did you know that?"

"No, I didn't know that," replied Tom. "I could use that information in a pub quiz," he thought to himself, but didn't wish to offend his amateur guide with sarcasm.

Having chained his bike, Dirk wished Tom a good stay and disappeared into the building. Ellen said that she had a class to attend but would be free to have lunch with him at 12:30 in the canteen. Tom agreed and after taking a leisurely look around the university found his way to the canteen a little earlier than agreed, to give himself time to see what kind of food was on offer. Ellen arrived from her class and spotted him immediately as she entered the

33

canteen. They took their food and joined a girl who had reserved seats for them at her table. The girl dressed in black with short dark hair and wooden jewellery greeted Tom, commented quickly to Ellen on the lecture they had just been to and then concentrated on her food before dashing off. Ellen said that she had been thinking about Tom's heroics that morning and would like to offer him a place on her sofa if he decided to stay another night in Rotterdam. While they were finishing off their food a girl dressed in purple with long plaited hair secretively gave Ellen a small package which she quickly put into her handbag and gave the girl some money. The two girls nodded and within seconds the girl had gone. Tom looked at Ellen, but she ignored his inquisitive look and pretended that nothing had happened. Finishing her coffee, she told him that she had classes until four o'clock and could meet him at the entrance just after that. As Tom left the building, he saw the tall figure of Dirk leaning against a tree. He tried to avoid eye contact, but Dirk saw him.

"You still have the rucksack on your back. Why don't you leave it somewhere? You could go and explore Rotterdam," he said as he walked towards Tom.

"I don't have anywhere to leave it," Tom replied.

Dirk said that he had a sports locker where he could leave his luggage. He led the way before Tom could think of an alternative. At 2.14 m Dirk was by far the tallest person Tom had ever spoken with. Dirk took Tom's haversack and placed it into his locker securing it with a padlock. He then took a map from his jacket pocket, made some marks on it and said,

"Here are some places you might like to see. You can keep it. It is a gift from me to you, as a Dutchman to an Englishman."

Tom thanked him and said that he would be back at around four o'clock. Feeling liberated without that weight on his back, Tom walked around Rotterdam taking pictures of interesting sights including a bridge and a place he understood to be called the White House near the harbour. It was a few minutes before four when he arrived back at the university where Ellen was already waiting for him.

"Have you seen Dirk?" he asked.

"Yes, I saw him about an hour ago. He's gone to Groningen to play in a volleyball match," Ellen replied, to Tom's dismay.

"I have to go there. He's got my luggage in his locker," said Tom.

"I'm afraid Groningen is in the north of the country," said Ellen trying not to laugh.

"Are you Tom?" asked an unfamiliar voice. And as Tom turned to face the voice, he saw a girl wearing a green tracksuit.

"Yes I am," he replied, not knowing what to expect. The girl explained that Dirk had had to leave earlier than planned and had given her the key to his locker asking her to find Tom, whom he knew would be meeting Ellen at around four o'clock, and give him his belongings. Tom thought how lucky he was that Dirk had remembered to leave his key before going off for the weekend, as he and Ellen walked towards her flat which she explained she had only just moved into having previously lived with her parents.

After having a cup of tea Ellen said that she needed to do some shopping, so they went to a shopping centre nearby where Tom looked around comparing prices to the UK while Ellen bought a few items including chicken, which she prepared with some rather tasty salad. Tom was still thinking about that mysterious package Ellen had received earlier that day, so he decided to ask her about it.

"Oh, thank you for reminding me. I'm going to have to see if I have wrapping paper. It's a present for Ester, the girl at our lunch table. It's her birthday tomorrow. It was something I wanted to buy but couldn't find here, so my friend bought it from Amsterdam for me."

It was quite late when the doorbell rang. Ellen opened the door and after a brief conversation in Dutch, a slender shortish man with straight brown hair and glasses entered the room and said,

"Hi, I'm Ruudi, Ellen's boyfriend. I think it is not appropriate for you to stay here. I'll give you a lift to the station. You can take your train tonight instead of tomorrow morning."

Ellen, who by that time was standing behind him said, "I'm sorry, I told him that we are just friends, but he just doesn't like the idea of you spending the night here."

As Tom boarded the train to Hamburg, he thought to himself, "Now there's a relationship that's not going to last."

Tom found a compartment where he could lay out his sleeping bag hoping that he would not have to share the compartment with too many people. Five minutes into the journey there were already three people sitting opposite him, so he decided to lie down, and he was soon asleep. He had been aware of passengers coming and going and when he opened his eyes in the morning, he noticed that his three co-travellers had been replaced with four new faces and at the same time the door slid open and a man walked in gesturing Tom to make room for him. Tom rolled up his sleeping bag and placed it in its cover before going to the toilet where he brushed his teeth and had a shave. When he returned to his compartment there was a sixth person there, but there was not long to go.

Day 6 Saturday

The station at Hamburg was quite noisy, and Tom soon found himself looking for something to eat. At a nearby supermarket, he opted for a loaf of bread and some cheese, which he washed down with some orange juice on a park bench, but before he could finish, he felt a few drops of rain that increased rapidly and forced him into a shopping mall. Tom spent several hours looking around in shops comparing prices as usual. He was also interested to see how their technological goods compared with what he was used to back home. Tom liked the shops, but after several hours he'd had enough and decided to leave the shopping mall and see more of Hamburg. It was still raining but not as heavily as before. The grey skies made the city seem dull, but Tom wanted to see as much as possible and didn't mind a bit of rain. He walked for hours, going into shops and underground stations from time to time to see more and avoid the rain as much as he could. By late afternoon the breakfast he had had on the park bench seemed like a distant memory, and so when Tom saw a McDonald's in one of the shopping centres, he was tempted to take the weight off his feet and refuel with a hamburger and shake. Once he had collected his order Tom picked a seat at a table occupied by a young German girl. At least he assumed she was German. As he watched the native Hamburgers eating hamburgers, he could not resist but ask. "Are you a Hamburger?"

"Yes, I am," she replied with a smile.

Tom couldn't be sure whether she was smiling in recognition of his joke or just being friendly. He regretted the joke and felt a bit embarrassed, but it was too late to withdraw the joke, so he turned it into a serious question by asking factual questions about the city. Tom also wanted to know if she knew where he could find cheap accommodation. Christina was quite an attractive girl but the small mole above her top lip made Tom feel a bit uncomfortable at first. She talked with passion about her city, but said that she didn't know much about accommodation in Hamburg as she had never been a tourist there. While they were talking, a man approached her from behind, leant over, put a hand on her shoulder and as she turned their lips met briefly. She said something to him in German that included the name Tom.

The man shook hands with Tom and said, "I'm Klaus." He then joined the short queue to order his food.

"We got engaged last week," said Christina joyfully.

Klaus joined them with his food, and they sat there eating until they had finished and were ready to go. When leaving, Christina and Klaus held hands and spoke German while Tom tried to give them their privacy by staying in the background.

Christina then turned to Tom and said, "We are driving to Hannover to stay with the parents of Klaus, but Klaus knows someone you can stay with for one night if you want."

Klaus said that he would take Christina home to get ready for the trip while taking Tom to where he would be spending the night. The place was quite a large second floor flat near the harbour. Klaus handed Tom over to Stefan who was one of the young Germans who were sitting on cushions on the floor. There were three of them to start with, but Tom could hear that there were others in various rooms in the flat who appeared from time to time.

"We are all students," said Stefan, "It is almost free for us to live here. We can't afford anything more modern. It suits us for now."

There was a girl sitting adjacent to Tom, wearing jeans and a dark blue t-shirt with something German written on it. She didn't speak any English and in fact, hardly said anything in her own language as she spent most of the time reading a book and drinking tea. The other person in the room was a guy who seemed very laidback and only spoke when Stefan couldn't find the right word in English. Stefan spoke about his political views which Tom found interesting at times, but difficult to follow his logic. A pretty girl with short blond hair walked into the room and sat next to the girl with the book. The laidback guy had already left the room. The two girls spoke briefly in German before also leaving the room. Almost as soon as the girls had left, a man who seemed quite a bit older than the rest of the occupants walked into the flat carrying three buckets of paint, said something to Stefan in German and walked into the kitchen. Stefan followed him and Tom could hear his name being mentioned. A few minutes later, while Stefan could be heard tinkering in the kitchen, the man came out and introduced himself to Tom as the owner of the flat.

"What do you do?" the man asked.

Tom said that he was a university student from England. The man said that Tom could spend the night there.

"These people are all students," said the man. "They can stay here for free because they are renovating the apartment for me. The academic year is over, and their work is almost done."

"Will you start charging them rent if they want to stay longer?" Tom asked.

The man gave Tom a stern look and replied, "It's not about the money right now. This is an investment for the future. It's for my boys. It'll give them a reason to stay and study in Hamburg if they have somewhere to live rent-free. I don't want to lose my boys. I lost my youngest son for over a year after a day at the zoo. One day I took my two sons, who were six and nine years old at the time, to the zoo where we saw lots of animals as expected, but also my boss. I had been working for that man for about ten years. Even my wife had worked in the same small company, but when we started a family, she decided to stay at home and bring our sons up while doing some freelance work from home.

"The next day when I was at work, my boss walked into my office, shook his head with a wink and said, "That's a fine boy, that Jacob. He must be about 6 years old now. The other one's OK too, but Jacob is something special." About 15 minutes later he came back to my office and said, "Why don't you come over to my house this evening at six o'clock to see my collection of stamps. You can get my address from my secretary. You don't need to bring Jacob. He'll just get in our way." I had no interest in stamps but could hardly refuse my boss's invitation. At six o'clock I drove into his driveway and was greeted by him at the door. He showed me in and asked me to follow him upstairs into a large room that looked like a study room. There was a big desk with a computer and a leather chair. He had several bookcases full of books and in the middle of the room was a round table and two armchairs. On the floor, there were a pair of dumbbells and an exercise bike with a dressing gown hanging over the handlebars. He said, "I know you never touch alcohol, so I won't offer you any. " As I stood there wondering why he had made such a totally incorrect statement, he walked to one of the bookcases and pulled out a stamp album which he placed on the table in the middle of the room and opened to a seemingly random page. "Here are my stamps", he said, "I even have some from Mauritania. My aunt knew a sailor who once went there. But you are not here to see my stamps." He then closed the album and opened a briefcase that was on the same table. It was full of banknotes. "This is for you," he said, "in exchange for Jacob. Of course, we will do it legally. My lawyer can be here in 35 minutes. You can sign Jacob over to me and the briefcase will be yours, and the money too." I looked at him in amazement, waiting for him to admit that this was some kind of joke, but it seemed that he was expecting me to give him a serious answer. As I walked away shaking my head in disgust, he shouted out, "You have until midnight to make your mind up. After that, I withdraw my generous offer and you will get nothing."

"I didn't mention anything to my wife when I got home as I thought it was too absurd and quite sick too. The next day at work he acted as if nothing had happened. When I was at home in the evening the doorbell chimed and my wife opened the door. It was my boss who walked straight into the living room where I was sitting and announced, "I have come to take Jacob, and my money offer has expired, so you will get nothing." I looked at my wife for a reaction, but with an unchanged expression, she took a step towards him and said, "Yes, he is the biological father of Jacob, and we want to be a family. " They had decided to take Jacob with them that night and threatened to tell Jacob that I was not his real father if I stood in their way. I knew this would damage the boy psychologically and so I reluctantly let them go. The boys were confused and didn't want to be separated, but we made it seem like it was a good thing. My wife showed no emotions when she left without one of her sons, but I was very sad without Jacob and many nights I almost cried. It goes without saying that I did not turn up for work again and after a short break, started my own company. A lot of my colleagues joined me from the old company, which started to go downhill, while my business was thriving.

"Over a year had passed and one night when my eldest son had gone to a friend's house for a sleepover, I was lying in bed thinking of Jacob whom I had not seen for several weeks. I heard what sounded like a wolf howling and remember thinking that we didn't have any wolves in the neighbourhood and thought that it must have been a dog or a cat, or some other 4-legged animal. The next thing I remember, I was woken up by some noise in the house. I quickly closed my eyes pretending to be asleep. A few minutes later I felt the presence of someone in the room standing over me. I opened half an eye and saw the blade of a knife gleaming in the moonlight. A figure in black was standing there. A small figure that I recognized as my beloved Jacob. He flung his arm around me and said, "You are my real Papa, not that man." He had run away and somehow found his way to me after walking for several hours in the middle of the night oblivious to the possible dangers. He had opened and climbed through a kitchen window with the help of a knife he had brought with him and was on his way to his bedroom but wanted to see me before going to sleep. He was clearly exhausted, so I got him ready for bed and tucked him in. He fell asleep almost immediately and I sat by his bed looking at his innocent face wondering what he must have gone through. I thought that under the same circumstances at his age I would have probably done the same thing. Like me, he was adventurous and a risk-taker. He shared many of his facial features with my wife and looked nothing like me, but the more I thought about his behaviour the more I could see myself in him. His words echoed in my head, "You are my real Papa, not that man." I rose to my feet as if a weight had been lifted from my shoulders. When my wife told me that I wasn't Jacob's real father, I was so devastated that I didn't question her story. But now it was clear to me that Jacob was my son. I phoned my wife to say that Jacob was safe and with me. She hadn't noticed that Jacob was missing and was not happy that I had woken her up. When I asked her, she admitted that I was Jacob's real father and then hung up.

"I now had both my sons with me and was happy. My wife had filed for divorce, but when my lawyer mentioned that she had separated the two bothers by lying and had allowed a small boy who had only just turned eight to wander the streets after midnight, she probably thought that she would not be given access to the boys and had more to lose than gain if the divorce went through, so about two months later she called me and asked if we could get back together. By that time, I had met the blonde Monika with the big blue eyes. She was good with the children and could make a perfect boiled egg. That is the quality I admire most in a woman.

"Life was fun with the blonde Monika with the big blue eyes, until she started to develop an unhealthy interest in horses and began to spend less time with us. It became her dream to move to Argentina and breed horses, and as she had studied Spanish at university, it wasn't long before her dream became a reality, and she was out of our lives. Meanwhile, my wife had gone into her shell and had not been in touch with us or anyone else for almost two years. I heard rumours that she was travelling around India and some other countries. Even her parents weren't sure where she was. They never came to Hamburg but were occasionally in touch with their grandsons. We used to visit them in Dresden from time to time when we were a proper family. Then one day my wife suddenly returned and begged for forgiveness. She said that she had been going through a crisis and travelled to India to get away from things. It was there where she learned yoga and got deeply involved in meditation. She told me that in a meditative state she would disconnect from people and the material world and become part of nature, but she said that the more disconnected she was from everything and everyone else, the stronger her maternal connection with her sons became. She said that they were a part of her that she could not and did not want to forget. I could see that she had changed, and I felt a serenity in her voice and presence that had not been there before. I decide to take her back and I'm glad I did. We are a proper family now. The boys are 13 and 16 years old. We have said that they will always be welcome to live at home with us, but I am sure they will want their independence, so they can move into this apartment until they have enough money to buy their own properties, which I hope will be in Hamburg."

When the landlord left, Stefan, who had just returned from another part of the flat, showed Tom into a room. There was a large bed with a leopard skin cover over it and a single mattress on the floor with some bedding. He pointed to the mattress and told Tom that he could sleep there and leave in the morning. Shortly after Tom had got into bed the pretty blonde girl walked into the room and got into the big bed. Tom tried to make conversation, but the girl didn't speak any English.

A strong smell resembling cooked potatoes kept Tom awake for a while and he woke up to the same smell in the morning.

Day 7 Sunday

Tom thought he was dreaming; the pretty blonde girl was standing over his mattress totally naked. She was looking in the wardrobe for clothes to wear that day. Tom pretended to be asleep by keeping still as he peered at her from under the sheet hoping that she would take her time in making her choice of clothing. The girl got dressed and left the room. Tom put on his clothes and within minutes he had left the building. All the occupants were still asleep in their rooms. The sky was cloudy and the smell of cooked potatoes was even stronger than before. Tom knew that the station was not far and he had just enough time to buy some chocolate, which he hoped would keep him going until Copenhagen. On the train, after brushing his teeth and shaving, Tom returned to his window seat and took out his book of European timetables to plan his itinerary for the next week or so. He wasn't sure which route to take through Scandinavia. He looked at various times and the map and sat back in contemplation when a girl asked if she could borrow his timetable. She said that she was on her way home to Stockholm and wanted to see which train she should take from Copenhagen. Her name was Pia, and she had short reddish-brown hair. She told Tom that she had been travelling around Europe and accidentally left her timetable at a youth hostel in Dusseldorf. She said that she had had a great time but was glad to be on her way back.

"I was very shy when I set off from Stockholm," she said. "I really couldn't have done it without my friend Ulrika who had Interrailed before. We kept each other company and hardly talked to anyone else until we met two Italian men. They were both very good-looking and charming but tried to get intimate with us very quickly. They thought that just because we were Swedish, we would jump into bed with them. Unfortunately, one of them stole my money and credit card. I immediately put a stop to my credit card and had to borrow money from Ulrika to survive. As it happened Ulrika didn't get time to spend much of her money because she fell ill with food poisoning in Greece and was flown back to Stockholm. I don't know why they didn't treat her there in Greece. Anyway, she's OK now, so it was good that she went back to be with her family. Since then, I had to travel alone, and I met a lot of interesting people I would probably not have met had I been travelling with Ulrika. I met a girl in Bosnia who was an artist. She invited me to stay with her. She was such a positive person and I very much enjoyed being with her, until the third day when she suddenly turned nasty. It was as if she was a different person. She said some bad things about me, and I had to leave. At first, I felt hurt but now I just feel sorry for her. This can't be normal. I hope she gets the help she needs."

Pia continued, "I met this guy in Greece who took me on his boat. I found out that he was married and just wanted to take nude photos of me. He wasn't an artist, just a pervert. Luckily, he wasn't violent and let me off the boat when I told him that I was not interested. I suppose he was afraid that I might tell his wife."

"Quite an adventure you've had," said Tom. "Are you alright for money?"

Pia nodded her head and smiled. "I wish everyone was as kind and generous as you," she said.

He had not intended to help her financially but was happy to take credit for it. Tom told her about the pickpocket in Rotterdam and how he had had to go to the hospital to get his finger seen to. To Tom's surprise, after a brief stop, the train boarded a ferry. Tom and Pia followed the other passengers off the train onto the car deck where there was at least one other train and some lorries. A button opened a heavy sliding door and everyone ascended the narrow stairs leading to the lobby. Tom and Pia looked around in the tax-free shop and small restaurant and then went on deck to intake the fresh sea air and scenery before finding their way back to their train. By the time they reached Copenhagen Tom was starving, as he had not had a chance to eat his German chocolate. Pia told him that she had decided to take the next train to Stockholm, as she had already seen Copenhagen and was feeling rather tired. She recommended an eating-place in a pedestrian street near the station where they had kebab-style chicken sandwiches. She also told him that there was a place at the station where travellers with Interrail tickets could rest and leave their luggage. After finding her platform, just before getting on her train, she scribbled something down and handed it to Tom saying,

"This is my address; if you are ever in Stockholm you are welcome to stay with me." She then gave Tom a hug and climbed into the train.

Tom found the travellers' centre at the station and left his luggage there. He was told to exit the station at the Tivoli end to find the pedestrian street. It was a sunny day with a slight breeze and Tom soon had the sandwich that had been recommended to him. He continued to walk away from the station enjoying watching various street entertainers and looking in some shops but then decided to go back to the station and see if he could find somewhere cheap to stay for the night. As he entered the station, he noticed a man grab an old busker's accordion and run. Tom immediately gave chase and as he got closer to the man, began to think how he should tackle him without jeopardising the accordion. He then noticed some stairs down to the other exit which the man was running towards and thought it would slow the man down sufficiently for him to be caught, but the man bypassed the stairs and to Tom's astonishment ran straight into the police station. Minutes later the man emerged with two police officers whom he took to the busker. The man had asked the old busker if he could give him change for a large banknote. The busker had taken the man's money and refused to give him any change. Tom thought it was lucky that he hadn't tackled the man who turned out to be innocent. He decided to go down the stairs and explore the other side of the station. That side was less appealing, and he soon passed some sex shops, but when he saw a street with hotels, he thought they might suit his budget. Tom was by no means from a poor family, but he was afraid that the extra money his father had given him might not last a whole month. He did have a credit card to fall back on, but he knew that he would have to repay it and didn't want to run up a debt. Therefore, as he approached the reception desk at the first hotel, he knew that it was more a question of curiosity. He also knew that the other hotels would charge roughly the same amount, so when he heard two young men speaking in an Irish brogue wearing hotel uniforms, he asked them if they could get him a discount. The Irishmen laughed and said that they were mere chambermaids and had no influence there. They asked Tom how long he was staying there and told him that they were university students from Dublin who had come over to earn some money and see Copenhagen. They said that they were staying at a dormitory and told Tom that if he didn't get a better offer and wanted to stay with them, he could meet them at five o'clock when they finished work. Tom went back to the station and Interrail centre where he had left his luggage.

The receptionist, who had already seen his ticket recognised him and welcomed him back. She pointed to a table covered with books and said that he could take one with him or leave one of his own books that he had finished reading.

"The scheme was introduced by an Englishman just like you, many years ago," she said.

The only book Tom had taken for his journey was his book of train timetables and so far, he hadn't needed to occupy himself with any books. Below the reception area was a large room with benches and tables where young travellers were resting and eating. Tom took his belongings and sat at a table, which he shared with a brown-haired girl wearing jeans and a dark blue blouse. There was also a man with dark hair wearing a black sleeveless shirt, but he was putting his things together and soon left.

"Strange guy," the girl said as soon as he was out of earshot. "He took a picture of a woman out of his wallet, looked at it lovingly and kissed it three times before putting it on the table and stabbing his knife through it. He then took some bread, cheese and a tomato out of his bag and made a sandwich using the same knife. He told me that it was the girl he loved, and like this he could feel close to her when he was eating." The girl then began to eat a sandwich.

"I hope that guy didn't make you this Sandwich," said Tom with a smile.

The girl laughed, "I'd have to be a lesbian to eat a sandwich made from another girl's picture". Tom found her sense of humour a bit odd.

"Where are you heading?" He asked, changing the subject.

"I'm going home to Sweden," she said. "I still have a week left on my Interrail but need to get back home."

"I'm planning to go to Stockholm on Tuesday. Is it a nice place?" Tom asked.

"Yes," she replied, "but not as nice as my hometown Gothenburg."

She then told Tom that she needed to go upstairs and asked Tom if he would like to join her. As soon as they were in open air the girl took a packet of cigarettes from her handbag, lit a cigarette, offering one to Tom at the same time, and took a deep puff. "My name's Helena," she said, exhaling the smoke away from Tom realising that he was not a fan of cigarettes. Tom had never been attracted to girls who smoked. He didn't mind Helena smoking, though he was glad when it was over and they could talk freely without the fear of him inhaling unwanted smoke. Tom and Helena walked around talking about the places they had been to. She told him that she had spent some time in Istanbul with a friend. She said that she accidentally made quite a bit of money when she exchanged her Swedish money but was given the Swiss rate by mistake but unfortunately lost a lot of that money when she bought a very expensive leather jacket which would have been a good deal had it not turned out to be fake. She explained that her friend had decided to see out the full month on her ticket and that is why she was travelling alone from Austria while her friend travelled down to Spain. Suddenly Tom noticed the time. It was almost five o'clock and he had to meet the two Irishmen outside the hotel if he wanted to stay with them. He rushed back with Helena to the centre where he had left his luggage. Helena wrote her address on a piece of paper and told him that she would like it if he changed his mind about Stockholm and visited her in Gothenburg. Tom thanked her and dashed up the stairs while pulling the straps of his orange haversack over his shoulders. Luckily the hotel was

51

not far from the station, but by the time Tom got there it was just gone five and the Irishmen were not there. He took a deep breath and sighed looking towards the end of the street to perhaps catch a glimpse of them before they turned the corner, but there was no sign of them. He stood there for a while until he noticed two women come out of the staff room and leave the hotel. He asked them if they knew the two Irishmen who worked there.

"You probably mean Jack and Everett. They'll be out soon," one of them replied. No sooner had she uttered those words than the two Irishmen appeared. They greeted Tom and off the three of them went. They took a local train and got off at a station that had been recently renovated. Outside the station was an open area with tall buildings on the other side. Shortly after passing a playground, they entered a building and went up to the third floor where there was a long corridor with lots of rooms and a communal kitchen. Jack unlocked one of the doors and they walked into a room that had two beds, a chair and a desk. Tom put his haversack up against the side of the desk and looked out of the window.

"How long have you been here?" he asked.

"This is our second month," replied Everett who was a short man with red curly hair. Jack, who was quite a bit taller with dark brown hair and rosy cheeks continued,

"When we first arrived, we didn't have a job or a place to stay. We walked into a hotel looking for a room, but they thought we had gone there for a job interview. They were short-staffed and happy to offer us work. They also gave us freeboard for one night and helped us find rented accommodation through the local paper. Our landlord who was Greek had thrown two mattresses on the floor in his spare room that he was renting short term to desperate tourists. He kept on telling us that we were not allowed to enter his chicken. We never told him that the word he was trying to say was kitchen. We had a lot of laughs behind his back, but luckily by the second week, we had met Morten who told us about this place." While Jack was talking, Everett had gone to the kitchen to prepare food.

Jack said, "Let's go to the kitchen. It's also the TV room."

In the kitchen, two Danes were watching a football match on television and having a heated discussion in Danish. All Tom could understand was the names of some footballers and what sounded like the name of Scooby-Doo being thrown in from time to time. By then he was starting to get hungry and was wondering what Everett's culinary masterpiece would be. A few minutes later it arrived. It was a pot of potatoes. The two Irishmen tucked in, but Tom only joined in when he was offered butter and salt with the potatoes.

It was still quite early when Jack and Everett knocked on a door further along the corridor, and moments later a tall Dane with fair hair appeared carrying a mattress which they placed on the floor in their room. It was Morten, the person who had saved them from the chicken-loving Greek landlord. He introduced himself to Tom as he returned with a pillow. Morten asked Tom what he was planning to do in Denmark, but Tom's answer was soon interrupted by Everett who said that they needed to get to sleep, as they had to get up early for work the next morning. Morten went to the TV room while Tom reluctantly got ready for bed. It was much too early for Tom to go to sleep. He was not at all tired. Or at least that's what he thought.

Day 8 Monday

The next thing Tom knew, he was waking up to the sound of the alarm on someone's watch. The three early risers got ready and convened in the kitchen for tea and cheese sandwiches. Everett told Tom that they started work at seven o'clock six days a week until they returned to university on September fifth. He said that their next day off was on Thursday, which they could spend together with him if he was still there. Tom said that he would take his luggage but return to them in the evening if he had not decided to move on. Tom enjoyed the early morning fresh air as they walked briskly to the station to catch the train into town. As Tom said goodbye to his Irish friends at the entrance to the hotel where they worked, he was torn between going to Stockholm and spending another day in Copenhagen, but knew that he didn't have to make his mind up straight away. It was a nice sunny day and having slept well and just eaten, he was full of energy. He walked around town, and as more and more shops began to open for business, he found himself walking in for a look around, converting the prices into his own currency. He preferred department stores where he could wander around without being approached by shopkeepers. In one of the department stores, while he was checking the quality of a pair of jeans, he noticed an elderly woman eyeing him up. She walked towards him with a shirt in her hand.

"Excuse me," she said; "I noticed you standing here. I hope you don't mind, but I think you are the same size and build as my nephew. I want to buy him this shirt. Would you mind trying it on?" Tom tried it on and it was a perfect fit. Tom noticed the price as the woman thanked him and began to walk towards the till to pay for it. He remembered that he had seen a very similar shirt for much less.

"I know a place where you can get it for about half this price," he said quickly, looking around to make sure no one else had heard him. "It's not far from here. I can take you there."

"OK, we can try," said the woman while putting the shirt back. As they left the shop, Tom hoped that he would be able to find the shop straight away and that he had not got the price wrong. As soon as the woman saw the shop, she said, "Yes, of course. I had forgotten about this shop." The old lady bought a shirt that she liked much more than the original one for a fraction of what she had been willing to pay at the first shop.

"I know a place that serves very nice herbal tea. We can share a pot if you would like to join me," she said.

At the tearoom, which was run by a friendly soft-spoken woman, the old woman chose a table for two by the window and ordered a pot of tea. She introduced herself as Grethe, and while calmly drinking her tea, asked Tom about his reason for being there and his plans for the future. She also asked him about his family, telling him that she was sure his mother was already missing him a lot. She told him that she liked gardening and often made her own herbal tea.

"I'm having a few people over today. Why don't you come too? Two of the ladies are going to English conversation classes. I'm sure they'd love to meet you." Tom accepted her invitation and after finishing their tea, they went to the bus stop and waited for the right bus to arrive. As Tom put his hand into his pocket to pay the driver for his ticket, Grethe told him that she had already paid for him with her travel card. The bus ride took about 15 minutes and Tom enjoyed watching the buildings and streets go by as they reached the suburbs. Grethe's house was not far from the bus stop and as they entered, Tom felt a warm homey feeling. Tom put his haversack next to the coat rack and Grethe asked him to take his shoes off. They then proceeded into the living room where Grethe told Tom to make himself at home while she went into a room that he assumed was her bedroom. She returned moments later wearing a tracksuit bottom and a white t-shirt. She opened the french windows in the living room and pointing to the garden, said, "I have planted all these myself." She then put on a pair of old trainers and went into the garden inviting Tom to put his shoes on and join her. She showed Tom the plants she seemed most proud of. Tom was impressed that she knew all their names in English. She then pottered about a little while informing Tom of the nutritional and even medical benefits the various plants had. She was an energetic healthy-looking woman; young at heart, aged only by her white hair. In the kitchen, she chopped some tomatoes that she had just picked and made some cheese and tomato sandwiches, which they had with a cup of herbal tea while telling Tom about her favourite places in Denmark. She then told Tom that she was in the habit of taking a nap in the afternoon and asked Tom if he liked cycling.

"I have an extra man's bike you can use, but please don't forget to lock it up if you leave it somewhere," she said handing him a key ring with two keys. "The other key is to my front door in case I am still asleep when you get back."

Tom had not cycled for ages and felt exhilarated by the breeze as he zoomed along the clearly marked cycling lanes. He cycled to a shopping mall that he had passed on the bus earlier that day, locked up the bike and walked in. He was attracted to a library and amazed at how many books there were in English. There was also a bank in the shopping mall where he looked at the exchange rate before continuing on his bike, cycling away from the main road until he reached a football pitch where he stood and watched for a while. He hadn't noticed the passing of time. It was already five o'clock. "Surely Grethe was awake by now," he thought. He cycled back speedily as he still had a train to catch later that evening.

As he opened the front door, he could hear the sound of chattering in Danish and recognised Grethe's voice. He followed the voices into the garden and was greeted by Grethe.

"Hello Tom, come and meet my friends. This is Barbara, Bea and Mrs Kristofersen. She's 92." The three ladies began to ask Tom about his time in Denmark while Grethe unfolded a garden chair for him. She then went into the kitchen and moments later called her guests to go in and help themselves. She had baked a large tray of pizza. Tom had sensed the tasty smell of something in the oven as soon as he had walked through the front door after his cycling. Grethe explained that the pizza was in four parts consisting of different toppings to cater for everyone's taste. They all took their pizza to the garden. There was a bowl of salad too, and two bottles of homemade wine.

"You will be staying tonight, won't you?" asked Grethe.

Tom was relieved that he wouldn't have to rush to the station. He was enjoying his time with the old ladies, eating pizza and sampling homemade wine. It was a relaxing evening for them all, talking about their hobbies and passions. Barbara, the smallest of them all, with a pointy nose that made her look even more like a mouse, had a passion for crosswords and Agatha Christie books and felt a bond with Tom who was from the same country as her favourite author. Bea, who was not as slender as the others and seemed keen to point out that her husband was a lawyer, told them all about her recent trip to Brazil and showed photographs though she was not in any of them herself except for one where she was standing by a taxi outside Kastrup airport in Copenhagen. She said with excitement that during her two-week stay in Brazil she had met someone she was pretty sure was an alien as he spoke with an accent different from other Brazilians she had met. Tom raised his eyebrows but then realised that by alien she probably meant foreigner and decided not to be the one to question her. Though he still could not understand why she found meeting a foreigner in Brazil so exciting. The 92-year-old Mrs Kristofersen, who mentioned her age several times probably due to pride rather than dementia, was quite tall and slim with a kind-looking face. She said that she lived on the ninth floor and swam almost daily. It was quite late when the three old ladies began to make their way to the front door. When they had all left, Tom suddenly noticed that his haversack had disappeared from next to the coat rack.

Grethe opened a door and said, "This will be your room."

It was a tidy room with a bed, a bedside table, a desk and a bookcase with neatly arranged books. Tom saw his haversack leaning against his bed. It must have been in the way when Grethe's guests were arriving. Tom noticed a book in advanced computer programming.

"Does this belong to your son?" he asked.

"No, I don't have any children. I've never been married" she replied. She looked into the distance with sadness for a while, deep in thought before continuing,

"I was nearly married once. His name was Peter. He was tall with beautiful blue eyes and such a great

58

personality. We had so much fun together. He was very adventurous, which was good until he decided that he wanted to climb the Himalayas. He said that he wanted to marry me on his return. We were going to travel around Africa as part of our honeymoon and then start a family when we got back. He was a writer, so he could make money while travelling. The day before he left for the Himalayas, I gave him a heart-shaped locket with my picture in it. Three weeks into the expedition news came that he had become separated from his group in severe weather and was missing. A huge search party was formed and a week later his frozen body was found. As we were not married, I had no legal claims on his personal effects, but I begged them to return the locket to me. About a month later I received the locket that was the only tangible memory I had of him. They said that they found it clinched in his frozen hand. I opened it with love and sorrow, but to my shock and horror, I saw a picture of another woman in place of mine. I didn't know which was worse; losing the man I loved or learning that I never had him in the first place. My curiosity soon got the better of me and I tracked down the woman in the picture.

"At first, I observed her from a distance with hatred, but then decided to confront her. She burst into tears when I introduced myself. She said that they had been married for almost two years when he died, and among his personal effects that she had received was a letter he had written to her explaining that he had fallen in love with me and wanted a divorce so that he could marry his true love. When I told her about the locket, she said that the night before his departure she had caught him looking at what she thought was an empty locket. When he saw her looking at him, he said that he had bought the locket so that he could take a picture of her with him on his expedition.

What Peter was not to know was that his wife was pregnant. I kept in touch with her until her death a few years ago. I am godmother to their son Poul who is a grown-up man now. He works with computers in Odense and visits me when he can. The shirt I bought yesterday was for him, not my nephew. He's like a son to me. He's not really my son, but he could have been." Grethe sighed, "Life's so complicated, but at the same time so simple. All that matters is love."

She then tried to change the mood by asking Tom if he had any laundry that needed to be done. That night, before falling asleep, Tom thought about how Grethe must have felt and what he himself would have done.

Day 9 Tuesday

The next morning, Tom woke up to the chirping of birds. Grethe was sitting on the floor in the living room meditating, with his clean laundry neatly folded on the table behind her. He took his clothes to his room and quietly went to the bathroom where he took a shower, shaved, and removed the bandage from the finger he had injured in Rotterdam. He then continued packing his things in his room until he heard Grethe moving around in the kitchen. She was preparing breakfast, which they had with freshly squeezed orange juice. Grethe was sad to see Tom leave, but she knew that he had to move on.

It wasn't long before Tom was at the main station in Copenhagen waiting for the train to Stockholm. On the train, he chose a compartment and put his luggage up on the rack. A middle-aged woman and a little boy of about ten walked into the compartment with their luggage. They didn't speak English and Tom didn't recognise their language. Just before the Swedish border, Tom decided to find someone to talk to, so he started to walk towards the rear of the train. In the next car, he saw some backpackers and sat in their company chatting for a while until the train stopped. He asked them to keep his seat for him while he went to get his luggage from the other car on the train, but the doors between the two cars were locked. He watched in horror as the front part of the train began to move, leaving the rear of the train behind. He could see the young boy from his compartment watching him through the glass in the locked door and tried to make him understand by gesturing that he should keep an eye on his luggage. When it became clear that the part of the train with his luggage would not be returning, Tom began frantically looking for the conductor who told him that unlike Tom, his haversack was on the train to Stockholm. He said that he would contact the train driver and ask him to put Tom's haversack off at the next stop where it could be collected. By the time Tom had arrived at the station where he was to pick up his luggage, three hours had passed. As he neared the lost luggage office, he saw his orange haversack looking lost and lonely without him. He ran to pick it up, but the man in charge stopped him and asked for proof of ownership. He told the man to look in the front pocket where he would find Tom's passport.

Once reunited with his haversack, Tom realised that he would have a long wait for the next train to Stockholm. There was, however, a train leaving for Gothenburg shortly. Helena had recommended Gothenburg and invited him to visit her. "So maybe it was meant to be," he thought. He had been torn between Stockholm and Gothenburg, and as he took his seat on the train to Gothenburg, he felt happy to follow his destiny. It was late afternoon, early evening when Tom arrived at Gothenburg station and began to ask for directions showing the piece of paper with Helena's address. He was directed to a house in an affluent part of town, and as he rang the doorbell, his heart pounded. Would she be the one to open the door? Was she expecting him? The door opened and a young girl stood there with long brown hair looking at Tom who introduced himself and asked for Helena. The girl said that Helena had been expecting him, but her little sister Lotta had been taken ill and everyone was at the hospital. She said that she would take him to a hotel where Helena would meet him. The girl took Tom to a hotel in town and left him there to wait. He sat in the lobby looking at his watch from time to time until a figure dressed in black wearing dark sunglasses appeared.

It was Helena who said in a trembling voice, "I'm sorry but my six-year-old sister passed away a few hours ago. She had cancer. This is a terrible time for us. I need to be alone."

She then walked away not turning around even once to see Tom sitting there in shock. A few moments later he got up and walked slowly towards the railway station with a deep feeling of sympathy. At the station, Tom was looking at the timetable board, when he heard someone call his name. It was the girl with the long brown hair, who had answered the door at Helena's house, accompanied by a chubby blonde. The girl looked down as she spoke,

"I'm sorry," she said, "but you seem like such a nice guy I just had to tell you. Helena doesn't have a sister. She made this all up. She has done this before, but I've never been part of it, and I don't know why I did it this time. I thought it would be funny, but now I know what a sick joke it was. I'm not going to be friends with Helena anymore. I hope you will forgive me."

The two girls left Tom standing there flabbergasted. He found somewhere to sit and went deep into thought. He didn't notice the man with jet-black hair who sat next to him until the man spoke.

"Are you OK? I saw those girls talking to you and it was as if you went into shock."

Tom was silent for a moment and then began to tell the man what had happened. The man sympathised with Tom but said that sometimes good things can come out of bad situations.

"One day back in Bolivia when I was hiking in the mountains, I met a businessman. We got to know each other and discovered that we had similar business ideas.

He was also impressed with my knowledge of computers and offered me a job in his company in Ecuador. He offered me a high salary and a place to stay. I was very excited about the prospect of moving to Ecuador, though my parents were sceptical. The day came and I packed my bags and left my hometown for a new life in Ecuador. When I arrived at the address the man had given me, I was told that he was away on business and wouldn't be back for another three weeks. He had not mentioned me to them and they were unable to contact him. I decided to find somewhere cheap to stay and wait for him to return. During this time, I met a young Finnish girl called Anneli who was working there as an interpreter. She gave me shelter, and while I was staying with her, she convinced me to further my education in Europe. I applied to several universities and was accepted here in Gothenburg where I am now studying Architecture. Anneli is back in Finland and we visit each other as often as we can. She was staying with me for a week and I accompanied her to the station this evening as she had to go back. I never found out what happened to the Ecuadorian man who had offered me work. After a month, I gave up waiting. But my journey from Bolivia to Ecuador wasn't a waste of time or money because in two years I should be an architect and, more importantly, I have met the woman I hope to marry."

The man said that his name was Nestor and told Tom that he could stay with him for a night if he wanted to catch the train the next day. Nestor took Tom to his dorm after buying a carton of milk on the way. His room was rather untidy. There were two dirty cups and plates on the table and the butter had not been put away in the fridge. But Tom, who was still living with his parents, except for when he was at university sharing with two other students, was envious of his independence. They had some crisp

Swedish bread and butter, for which Tom was thankful as the only food he had eaten since breakfast was some sandwiches that Grethe had made for him to have on the train. They chatted over a few beers until Nestor said that he needed to sleep because he had a class the next morning. Tom brushed his teeth, unpacked his sleeping bag, took a cushion and curled up on Nestor's small couch. He woke up several times during the night, haunted by the memory of Helena and her sick joke.

Day 10 Wednesday

After a small breakfast, Nestor showed Tom to the station on his way to university. Tom had decided to go to Norway and visit Stockholm on his way back. He had several hours to wait for his train to Oslo, so he thought it would be nice to look around town. He felt a bit uneasy knowing that he might at any moment bump into Helena. While looking in a shop window he felt a tap on his shoulder. He turned round to see two girls, one of them holding a map, which he immediately recognised to be his own, as he had written some things on it. The small map had fallen out of his back pocket when he was adjusting his haversack. The two girls were Marit and Andrea from Norway who were there on holiday and about to fly back that day. They had just bought some beer and were looking for a nice place to sit down and chill out. They asked Tom if he would like to join them, and as he had plenty of time to kill, he thought it would be a good idea to spend some time with them. They found a park where they sat down. Andrea had shoulder-length light brown hair and was the one who had planned the trip and was responsible for their itinerary while Marit with her long red hair and freckles seemed easy-going and quiet. Andrea said that they had been staying near Gothenburg with her brother, his Swedish wife and their two small children. She said that she still had not seen some of the museums she wanted to see.

"This is the first time I'm here independently. I did come over for the wedding, but there wasn't much time to do anything else, and I was with my parents and five years younger then, so I wouldn't have appreciated it as much as I do now. Having a brother here allows me to spend more

66

time here than if I had to pay for my accommodation. I've been told that if my brother's alarm had worked properly, there wouldn't have been a wedding, and I wouldn't be here now."

"Don't you mean if it hadn't worked properly?" asked Tom.

"No, I meant exactly what I said. My brother Nils graduated as an engineer from the University of Gothenburg and was planning to return to Norway. He had applied for a couple of jobs in Gothenburg but heard nothing from them and he told me that he was looking forward to moving back to Norway. The plan was to leave early in the morning and drive home to Norway, but his alarm didn't work and he overslept. By the time he woke up, had his breakfast and loaded his car, it was by no means early in the morning. He said that he sat in his car looking for the last time at what he had called home for the past years, watching familiar faces going about their routine lives that would soon be fading away in his memory bank. He was about to start the car when he noticed the postman delivering the mail. It was the usual time but a different postman. Nils decided to check the post before driving on to return the dormitory keys. He had received one letter, which he took back to his car and opened with great curiosity. It was from one of the companies he had written to for a job. They were offering him an interview on the completion of his degree. He told me that he couldn't remember how long he sat in the car, thinking what to do. On one hand he wanted to get back to Norway, but on the other hand, he didn't have a job to go to and he knew this was a good opportunity for him. He decided to go for the interview and went with confidence as he felt he was in a win-win situation. Not only did he get the job, but the company helped him with accommodation and within a week he was working and living in a flat quite near his workplace. Around the same time, a young girl called Elis moved into the flat below. Nils told me that he was happy in his new job and flat, but the most exciting thing in his life was Elis who was warm but distant, like a star. As he got to know her, it transpired that she had recently broken up with her boyfriend and didn't want to rush into a new relationship. She said that he had stood her up one evening when they were supposed to see each other. He had phoned and told her that he was very ill and could not get out of bed. The next morning, she had taken him some food, but he was not at home. She said that she felt betrayed and started to have negative thoughts about him. Being the 13th of the month made her feel even more strongly that something sinister was going on. When they finally met, she flew off the handle and they had a row. He told her that he had taken a summer job, like a lot of university students do, and had forced himself out of bed because he needed the money. That is why he was not at home that morning when she dropped by with the food. By then a lot had been said that could not be taken back and the relationship seemed irreparable, so she decided to call it a day. She told Nils that she felt guilty about how she had ended her relationship with her ex-boyfriend but didn't regret it anymore. As Nils and Elis spent more and more time together, they became an item and eventually moved in together. One day when they were in town Nils noticed that Elis suddenly reacted uncomfortably, and so he asked her what was wrong. She discreetly pointed to a man and said that he was her ex-boyfriend. Nils recognised him as the young postman who had delivered that life-changing letter to him on the day he was about to leave. As he remembered the date, it dawned on him that if the postman had not dragged himself out of bed that day, he would have driven away to Norway without receiving the letter and Elis would have taken the food to her boyfriend and probably still been in a relationship with him. By delivering the letter that day, the postman was unknowingly delivering his girlfriend into the arms of Nils. Of course, none of this would have happened had my brother's alarm woken him up for him to leave early in the morning as planned."

Andrea was eager to see some of the museums she had not yet seen, but Marit wasn't interested so she stayed behind with Tom. By that time, she had drunk several beers and become quite talkative. She told him about Norway and how it doesn't get dark in the summer where she lives. She said that she lived so far north that trains didn't go there. Tom was fascinated and wanted to know more about Norway. They talked so much that Tom almost forgot that he had a train to catch. Marit wrote her address and phone number on Tom's map that she had picked up and said, "You really should come and visit me."

She couldn't go to the station with Tom, as she had to wait for Andrea, and he was in a hurry. Tom hadn't slept well on Nestor's small couch the previous night and soon fell asleep on the train, waking up half an hour away from Oslo. He went to the toilet to freshen up and on his return got talking to an American couple who had been to Norway many times before and recommended that he should visit Bergen. Tom was hungry when he reached Oslo and after seeing the high prices regretted not buying food for the next 24 hours while he was still in Gothenburg. He wasn't worried about finding a place to sleep as there was a train leaving for Bergen later that night arriving early the next morning. It was a nice summer's evening enjoyed by a multitude of people. Tom treated himself to a hotdog that did more to empty his pocket than fill his stomach. He got talking to an Egyptian family who said they loved it in Norway but still couldn't get used to the long dark winters. The man whose name was Gamal was very interested in politics and knew a lot about technology. He had been teaching Arabic and Maths there for 12 years and both his children were born in Norway.

He said, "When I first came here, all I wanted to do was learn the language. All my friends were foreigners who were in my Norwegian class. Several years into my stay here, I had learned the language and made a few friends but was still feeling lonely. I had met a lot of very nice Norwegian girls, but I felt that something was missing. They were just not right for me. I had been corresponding with a girl in Egypt whom I had never met, but our parents thought that we might be right for each other. I was going back to Egypt to visit my parents and told the girl that I would like to meet her. I remember how excited I was to finally meet her. We talked a lot and although we had quite a lot in common, it just didn't click. The next time we met, I told her that we didn't have a future together. The poor girl was heartbroken. I had never promised her anything, but she had been thinking about a future with me and was ready to move to Norway. She took rejection badly and showed her ugly side. I told her that she should not contact me anymore and asked my parents to tell her that I was out if she phoned. A few days later, she sent a friend round to ask me to reconsider. The girl was calm and tried to reason with me. She was kind and friendly, but I didn't change my mind. When I got back to Norway, I began to think about the mediator who had come to my home in Cairo. In fact, I couldn't stop thinking about her. I realised that for the first time I had fallen in love. I phoned home and asked my sister to find her telephone number. A few days later I gathered my courage and phoned her. Luckily it was she who answered the phone. My heart sank for a moment; I was almost tongue-tied, but after a moment's silence I did manage to talk. She was very surprised to hear my voice and admitted that she had been thinking about me too. Three months later I was back in Egypt; this time to ask for her hand and to marry her. As you can see, we have two children together and we are very happy. Norwegian people are very friendly, but I would be lost without my Egyptian wife. I really do need someone who understands me."

Just before midnight, the train left for Bergen, and as Tom lay out his sleeping bag and climbed into it, he thought about his own destiny and wondered how he would know when he has met the right girl. He waited for the conductor to check his ticket before making himself comfortable and closing his eyes for the night. He heard passengers entering his compartment, but pretended to be asleep, and soon was.

Day 11 Thursday

Early the next morning, Tom woke up to see the other passengers in his compartment already awake and eating. There were two girls quietly speaking in a foreign language that he recognised as being French.

"Bonjour," he said, exercising one of the very few French phrases he knew. The girls replied in English leaving Tom disappointed that his poor accent had not fooled them, but relieved that they could speak English. They were Marie and Sylvie who had travelled from Bordeaux where they were university students. They seemed to have plenty of food and asked Tom to join them. Marie was rather petit with short brown hair, while Sylvie was a bit larger in stature and had longer hair. Marie made Tom a sandwich while Sylvie explained that they had been staying with a Norwegian friend who had given them a lot of food to take. She said that she had never been to Bergen, but Marie had been there and liked it very much. Tom asked Marie where she had stayed, hoping for a tip.

"Well, it was a year ago. I had never been to Norway before, but I'd heard a lot of good things and so I thought it would be a good idea to spend some time here. I had been to the north and was on my way back south when I met a Norwegian girl who was going to Bergen, which was one of the places I had wanted to see. She invited me to stay with her and I was happy to accept her invitation. At the station, her boyfriend was waiting to drive us to their flat. He seemed like a nice person, and they were clearly very happy to see each other. Soon after we had arrived at their flat, they asked me if I wanted to go for a walk. I thought it was a good idea and got ready to leave with them, but then they gave me directions to some places they thought I might be interested to see and said that they would see me after six.

"I was a bit surprised because I thought they would go with me, but then they probably wanted to be alone. When I returned, they were happy to see me and welcomed me back. We talked for a while and then it was time to eat. We had chicken, potatoes and beans with wine. It was all going very well until suddenly in the middle of his chicken, the boyfriend yelled something in Norwegian and the girl shouted back at him. They got louder and louder and completely ignored me. I thought they were going to kill each other. I just couldn't stand it. I was so afraid I didn't know what to do, so I gathered my things and left. I could still hear them shouting on the third floor as I left the building. By that time, it was late and it had begun to rain. I walked aimlessly in the streets realising how foolish I had been to travel alone. It was raining even more, and I felt as if I had been walking for a long time when a car skidded next to me. It was the boyfriend's car, but the girl was driving. She pushed the door open and I got in. She was trembling and there was blood on her white t-shirt. "He'll never talk to me like that again," she said. "We have to find somewhere to hide from the police where we can sleep".

"It was too late for me to get out of the car. She drove nervously for several minutes until she turned into the woods, stopped the car and turned the lights off, and said that we should sleep there. I was terrified. I didn't want to sleep with a murderer in the car. I dozed off from time to time but each time I woke up expecting to see her with a dagger over my face. I didn't get much sleep, but she slept well, even though she was sleeping in the driver's seat and I was lying down on the backseat. In the morning, she was much calmer. She apologised for what had happened. She said that they had been having problems, but that row was the last straw. She couldn't take it anymore. She then took me to the boot of the car and opened it. I was dreading what I might see. Inside was a large spanner and a spare tyre, but lying under a thin blanket I saw her rucksack and two small suitcases. She told me that she had left him for good and was moving back home.

She said, "When you left, he got louder and began throwing things around. I get a nosebleed when I am very angry. This happened last night, but he didn't care. As you can see, I have some blood on my t-shirt. I locked myself in the bathroom waiting for my nosebleed to stop, and that is when I decided that I'd had enough. I quickly threw my most important belongings into two suitcases and took my rucksack that I hadn't even had time to unpack, and put them into his car and drove off. He could have reported the car as stolen. I would have been in trouble with the police, especially as I don't have a driver's license."

"She wanted to drive the car to the railway station, leave the keys under the seat and phone him to pick it up. I said that I had a license and would drive us to the station. On the way to the station, she told me that she was from a small island near Trondheim with a population of about 400 people and no police station, so she had driven many times without a license and was quite an able driver, but admitted that she had been feeling nervous because the circumstances were different. When we got to the station, she phoned him to pick up the car and we both took the train to Oslo where we would change trains and go our separate ways. We were sitting and talking for more than an hour when I quite innocently asked her if the row had been over the chicken. She suddenly jumped to her feet and said, "You're a very rude person." She then took her luggage and moved to a different part of the train. I never saw her again. So, I don't know anyone in Bergen and I don't know where we will stay, but we do have a tent. There are lots of nice places where we can put our tent up."

After roaming around Bergen for 45 minutes, taking in the scenery, Tom and the two girls noticed a tourist office. They decided to go in to take the load off their shoulders while getting some information. There were several backpackers there, mostly looking for cheap accommodation. While Tom and the girls were looking at leaflets and maps, they overheard a couple being offered free room and board if they could speak Esperanto. Marie and Sylvie looked at each other and quickly went to the desk announcing that they spoke Esperanto and asked whether what they thought they had heard was correct. They were told that they could stay with a family who spoke Esperanto if they could satisfy their hosts that they spoke Esperanto sufficiently. The woman behind the desk dialled a number and handed the phone to Sylvie who spoke with someone in Esperanto, making arrangements and taking notes at the same time. She then gave the phone back to the woman behind the desk and told her that they would be staying there for two days. Marie and Sylvie told Tom that he could have their food as they would not be needing it, wished him a bon voyage and left the office chattering in French. Tom continued walking around town until he found himself attracted to a hill where he sat on a bench mesmerised by the breathtaking view of the fjords. At the top of the hill, he found a secluded spot to pitch his one-man tent. He could not be overlooked but had a good view of the sea. He watched and sometimes waved as the occasional fishing boat or small ferry went by. It was perfectly tranquil there and he didn't feel the need to go to town until late afternoon when he had finished the food he had been given. He put his haversack in his sleeping bag inside his tent to make it look as if someone was sleeping there and went down to the shops. In one of the shops, he asked a girl with blond hair who was wearing a stripy red and white t-shirt to help him translate the ingredients into English to make sure he was not buying something that needed to be cooked. The girl told Tom what the words meant and how the food should be eaten. She suddenly recognised Tom as the man on the hill with the orange tent and told him that her name was Solveig and that she was travelling by boat along the Norwegian coastline. Tom told her that he had a very good view from where his tent was and offered to take her there. Tom had taken some pictures earlier that day but wanted to be in the pictures with the sea in the background, so he was pleased when Solveig agreed to go with him. She was impressed with the view and happy to take pictures of him, capturing the beauties of her country in the background. They talked about their travels on land and sea until Solveig said that she had to go back to the boat but said that she would return with some food that they could eat by his tent. Tom waited for almost an hour until he saw Solveig walking up the hill towards him, but she wasn't carrying anything. She told him that her father who was the captain of a fishing trawler had invited him to dine with them. She said that he should take his belonging with him and spend the night on the boat. Tom folded his tent, packed his haversack and followed Solveig down the hill. They walked for a while until they came to a row of boats and climbed aboard one of the bigger ones where Tom was introduced to Solveig's parents, brother and a few other people. Solveig's mother showed Tom to a small cabin and told him that he would be sleeping there. Solveig's portly father, who didn't speak English, seemed to know quite a few of the other captains. Her mother with her thin face and curly hair tried admirably to stretch her very limited knowledge of the English language to communicate and make Tom feel welcome. Solveig's ten-year-old brother, Kristian, spoke very little English but did occasionally come up with surprising phrases. Below deck, there were several small cabins, a toilet, and a living room with a kitchenette all joined together by a very narrow corridor leading to some steps up to the deck where they were to eat. Tom was surprised to find that the meal they were offering was sausage and mash, but later the fish arrived and that was what he had been expecting on a fishing boat. Solveig had told her family about Tom's plan to travel north, and they told him that they could take him as far as a place called Narvik. After the meal as they were finishing off their beer, a few drops of rain began to fall prompting them to clear the table and take cover below deck where they soon announced that it was time for bed as they wanted to get an early start the next day. Tom could hear the rain lashing down as he lay in his cabin, pondering what adventures the coming days would bring.

Day 12 Friday

The next morning, when he awoke, Tom felt the boat moving. As he stepped up on deck, he saw the sun shining, and Bergen was nowhere to be seen. The family had been awake for a while and had already eaten their breakfast. They greeted him and asked how he had slept. Solveig took him to the living room where his breakfast was waiting and told him to help himself. After breakfast, Tom went on deck and watched the Norwegian coastline go by, waving back at the children who were excitedly boat spotting. He waited for Solveig who had left him alone with his breakfast, but there was no sign of her. The mother kept Tom company for a while, talking about Norway and the fishing industry, dropping Norwegian words into the conversation to fill the gap in her English vocabulary. Solveig only resurfaced for lunch, saying that she had been busy and hoped that Tom had been enjoying himself. After lunch, Solveig cleared the table taking the plates down to be washed. Not long after lunch, the boat docked, and the captain stepped off to bring onboard two large boxes with the help of a younger man who stayed onboard talking as the boat continued its journey. As soon as the man noticed Tom looking at him, he went over and said, "Hi, you must be Tom. My name's Arne; I'm Solveig's uncle. My sister told me all about you. We are all very happy to have you here with us." Arne was only a few years older than Solveig. He had fair hair and was quite tanned.

"What kind of hobbies do you have?" asked Arne.

"Well, I like to play music and watch football."

"I prefer to play football and listen to music," said Arne. "Here in Norway, they show English football every week.

I watch it, but I enjoy playing for my local team even more. What instrument do you play?"

When Tom said that he liked playing the guitar, Arne laughed.

"I really wish I had been able to play the guitar two years ago when I was in Hungary. I met a beautiful girl called Kinga who was a singer in a band when I was in Debrecen. I heard that the guitarist had fallen out with the other members of the band, so I got talking to the manager of the band and just mentioned that I was a well-known guitarist from Norway. Of course, they had never heard of me, but then I'm sure they had never heard of any genuine Norwegian guitarist either. The manager asked me if I would like to audition and possibly join their band until they found a permanent guitarist. I told him that I had been drinking and would rather audition the next day when I was completely sober; and that I could only help out for three weeks.

"The next day I arrived with a bandage on my hand and told the manager that I would not be able to play the guitar for another three or four days. I told him how sorry I was to let him down but suggested that we could use a recording of the guitar sound, which they had on tape, and I would pretend to play the guitar. They were moving on to Bucharest the next day, so he agreed to take me. He introduced me to the band as a new temporary member. They were all happy to meet me and have me in their band as they thought I was a star in Norway. I was happy to be in the same band as Kinga, but the drummer was very friendly and hardly ever left me alone with her. On the third day, the manager told me that he was really happy because I would be taking the bandage off the next day. I told him that I was looking forward to it too. The next day I went to him with a sad face and told him that the

Romanian doctor had told me that I needed to keep the bandage on for another week. I continued to go on stage with them pretending to play the guitar.

"One evening the manager heard that there was a Norwegian man in the audience. He asked him if he had heard of me. Obviously, the man had not heard of me but didn't want to let on, so he said that he was a great fan of mine. After that, the manager became eager to sign a permanent contract with me. He offered me a lot of money, forgetting that I had not even auditioned. Of course, I couldn't accept his offer, so he offered me even more money, which I had to turn down. I was happy to hang around for a few weeks pretending to be injured while getting to know Kinga, but I couldn't sign a legal and binding contract, so I quit the band. The next day they found a temporary guitarist and reluctantly accepted my resignation. They asked me if I would dine with them one last time. It was my last chance to get close to Kinga, so I accepted the invitation. The drummer had a headache that night and left early, while the other members were talking among themselves. At last, I was alone with Kinga. We were getting along well, so I thought I would take it a step further and make a personal compliment. I told her that I enjoyed listening to her beautiful singing voice. Suddenly she looked at me like hell. She said that I was being sarcastic and making fun of her. She said that as a brilliant musician, I could surely tell straight away that she was only miming. She told me that the manager had asked her to do it because he wanted someone with more glamour than the original singer to attract a bigger crowd. I decided to come clean with her and admitted that I was only pretending to play the guitar. That just made things worse. She said, "Don't patronise me. I know you are a famous musician because you have been recognised by Norwegian tourists." She then got up, threw her napkin on the chair and stormed off. That was the last time I saw her."

Arne told Tom that they had a guitar on board and asked if he would play something for them. He agreed to play something that evening if he could first practise a bit in his cabin, as he was a bit rusty. After their evening meal, Tom went down to his cabin to fetch the guitar and returned with it, but sporting a makeshift bandage which almost had Arne falling overboard with laughter. Tom played the guitar to his appreciative audience, who blasted out the lyrics louder and louder the more they drank, well into the night that never seemed to get dark.

Day 13 Saturday

When Tom awoke the next day, he went straight to the living room area, where he saw Kristian and his mother with a woman whom he had seen several times but never spoken to. She looked to be in her 30s and wore red corduroy trousers with a white top. She was finishing her breakfast and soon left as Solveig entered and greeted Tom.

"You play the guitar well," she said, as she put an unopened bag of bread on the table for Tom in case he needed more.

"Where were you yesterday?" Tom asked.

"I had things to do while you were talking with my uncle, but I did come to listen to your music. It was very beautiful."

While Tom was still eating his breakfast, Solveig left, and once again when he went up on deck, she was not there. He could see the woman, who had been talking to Solveig's mother, engaged in conversation with the captain. The captain noticed Tom and greeted him with a wave while continuing to talk with the woman who was still a mystery to Tom. Moments later Arne joined Tom and told him that they would be reaching their destination that day. It was just after lunch that Tom noticed the boat slowing down and Arne told him that they would shortly be there. He went to his cabin to gather his belongings, and when he returned, the boat was about to dock, with all the passengers on deck. They all shook hands with Tom and wished him well in Norwegian or English. Solveig gave him a bag and told him to open it when he got hungry. Her mother gave him a doily with a map of Norway embroidered on it, which she said she had made herself. The captain gave him a Swiss Army knife that bore the name of his vessel, and not to be left out Kristian gave him a deck of cards.

He thanked everyone for their hospitality and left with Arne who said, "There are no trains here, but I will take you to the bus station where you have a bus leaving in 20 minutes. I'll take you there so that you don't miss it, because it's the only one leaving today."

Tom asked who the other people on the boat were.

Arne smiled and replied, "They are mostly family friends who travel with us and at the same time help us out. I'm sorry if they didn't talk to you much. They don't speak much English. We all have to learn English at school, but we can't all speak it. I have travelled a bit where I have had to speak English. Also, the captain knows a lot of tradesmen who hop on and off. They don't have to pay anything, but sometimes they bring things like a crate of beer or a leg of lamb for us to enjoy together. Sometimes the tradesmen leave goods onboard to be picked up by someone at another stop."

"What about the woman in the red trousers who was talking to Solveig's mother, who is she?" asked Tom.

Arne thought briefly, and after a quick look to make sure there was no one within earshot said, "Solveig's mother, my sister, used to have a drinking problem. She would drink on the rocks. I don't mean with ice. I mean literally on the rocks. With her husband working away from home days on end and the children at school, she would sit on a rock facing the sea and drink like that famous Danish virgin. She would always stagger home in time to meet her children from school, and did a good job as a mother, but we were worried about her health because she smoked a lot too. We were very happy when she agreed to check into a clinic for help. The woman you were asking about was a nurse at the clinic who went out of her way to help my sister. She spent a lot of her free time with my sister, saying that the worst thing for her was loneliness and boredom, which is probably what made her turn to the bottle in the first place. She said that sitting on a rock looking out to the sea meant that she was missing her husband, and of course she didn't drink when her children were around which showed that she cared about her family and was not a total slave to alcohol, though she was showing signs of depression. The nurse is quite a few years younger than my sister, but they became good friends, and she fixed her a part-time job at the clinic as a receptionist. She also recommended that she go to sea with her husband whenever possible. Thanks to the nurse, my sister is in control of her life and these trips have become quite an enjoyable family affair. My sister wanted to repay the nurse, so she came up with the idea that during her summer holidays the nurse could rent her flat to tourists and live on the boat. I don't know the nurse well, but my sister and the children like her a lot."

When Tom and Arne arrived at the bus station there was only one bus there. The engine was off but there were already some passengers on the bus. Arne asked Tom for the paper where Marit had written her address and got on the bus to show it to the driver. After a short conversation with the driver, Arne got off and handed the address back to Tom telling him that the driver would let him know when to get off. Arne then shook hands with Tom, wished him luck, and walked back towards the boat. Tom got on the bus and stopped to pay for his ticket, but the driver pointed to a piece of paper that Tom was holding with the map that had Marit's address on. Tom hadn't noticed but Arne had paid for his ticket. As he took his seat Tom could see Arne walking away in the distance and thought about how generous and kind these people had been. Shortly after the bus began its journey into the vast countryside, Tom looked to see what kind of food Solveig had given him. There was some apple pie, but also a letter that read: "My dear Tom, I can't begin to say how sorry I am to have treated you the way I did. When we met in that shop, I liked you straight away. I wanted to spend more time with you so I was glad when my parents said that you could travel with us. But when we were on the boat, I couldn't be alone with you. I was too nervous and shy. When you were up on deck, I was often in my cabin crying. That is why my mother called for my uncle to join us and make sure you were not alone. I hope you will find it in your heart to forgive me. With love, from Solveig."

Tom felt sorry for Solveig and a bit surprised, as he had not felt an attraction between them. The bus passed several small villages and even stopped at remote stops serving only one house until at one of the stops the driver indicated to Tom that they had arrived at his destination. Tom followed a path where the bus had stopped until he reached some old houses where he saw an old lady in her garden. He asked her for directions, holding up the address. She pointed to some modern houses near a lake and said something in Norwegian with a smile. As he got closer to the lake, he asked a rugged-looking man who was walking towards him, just to make sure he was going the right way. The man took a quick look at the address and said, "You want the three sisters; they live over there." Another man who was passing by overheard them and said, "The three sisters live in that white house."

As soon as Tom opened the gate and entered the garden of the modern white house, Marit opened the door and welcomed him with a smile. As he reached the front door, she was joined by a younger girl whom she introduced to Tom as her sister Astrid. Indoors he was shown to a large living room where he met their mother who greeted him and immediately inquired if he had eaten recently. The mother who had been watching television asked Tom about his favourite programmes and began to name some of the English programmes she herself enjoyed watching. Marit then led Tom to a room and said, "This used to be my older sister's room. She is living with her boyfriend now. You will sleep here tonight."

Later that evening her elder sister Hilde and her boyfriend Erik paid them a brief visit. Hilde was taller than Marit and had dark brown hair, and with their mother's fair hair Tom assumed that Marit's father must have been ginger. Marit had told him that her parents were divorced and that her father lived in another town with his new girlfriend. It seemed quite early when Astrid and then the mother went to bed. Marit explained that during summer, the sun never truly sets at night, and that is why it seemed early, but it was late and she wanted to go to bed. Tom found the midnight sun fascinating but difficult to get used to. He lay in the comfortable bed that smelled of fresh linen, pulled the sheets over his eyes and thought about his long day until his thoughts turned to dreams.

Day 14 Sunday

The next morning, when Tom woke up, Marit's mother was sitting on the veranda reading the Sunday paper while Marit and Astrid were still asleep. She noticed Tom and went in to offer him breakfast, but he said that he would wait for Marit. Tom walked onto the veranda and took a deep breath, enjoying the fresh air and view of the lake. Marit's mother joined him on the veranda and said, "Yes, it's nice here in the summer, but in the winter, it is dark the whole time and that lake is frozen. I feel quite lonely up here in the winter. It was better when my husband was still alive and the girls were younger. Now Hilde lives with her boyfriend and Marit is often in Tromso, so it's usually just me and Astrid here."

"I thought Marit said that you were divorced and that her father was living somewhere with his new girlfriend," Tom interjected, confusedly.

"No, no," she explained, "About six years ago Marit's cousin was getting married. We drove down to Bodo where the wedding was. It was a great wedding and we had booked a hotel for the weekend. My husband who was a heavy smoker would often leave us to go out and smoke. On that occasion I didn't mind because my aunt who lives in America had flown over for the wedding and I hadn't seen her for a while, so we had a lot to catch up on. I was so busy talking with my aunt that I didn't notice how long my husband had been gone. It was just gone ten when my aunt said that she was tired and wanted to go to bed. After she had left, I sat for a while and then went over to talk to one of the other guests when I noticed a passport on the floor. It belonged to my aunt, so I thought I would take it to her room. I could have given it to her in the morning, but I thought she might notice it was missing and worry. I went to the reception desk and asked which room she was staying in. They couldn't find her registered there. I asked them to check again but then one of the other guests heard me asking for her and told me that she was staying at another hotel because our hotel where the party was being held was fully booked. He said that he knew where the hotel was and could give me a lift. As I didn't know where my husband was, I let him give me a lift so that I could get to the hotel quickly. It was only a few minutes away and he said that he would wait for me in the car park. I asked at the reception which room my aunt was staying in and went up to give her the passport. She hadn't noticed it was missing but thanked me for bringing it over. I left her to continue getting ready for bed, but in the corridor I suddenly heard a voice that sounded very much like my husband's, coming from one of the rooms. I followed the voice and stood behind the door waiting for him to talk again. He wasn't talking much, just a word or two now and again, but I was sure it was him. I hoped with all my heart that he was having a drink and a chat with one of the guests. Then I heard a woman laughing. I knocked on the door; there was no answer. It was only after the third knock that he came to the door and opened it slightly to see who was there. He was shocked to see me. Before he could say anything, I pushed the door open and saw a woman in bed trying to cover her body. I didn't know what to say. I knew I wouldn't be able to control my tears, and I didn't want that woman to see me cry, so I left in a hurry and went downstairs. The man who had driven me there was in the car park waiting for me. I asked the receptionist to thank him and tell him that I would be going back to the hotel later. I needed to be alone and knew that if I went out, he would know that something was wrong. When he left, I went out of the hotel and started to walk towards my own hotel. It was then that I let myself cry like a child. I think nobody could see or hear me crying. Well, they didn't stop to help me; they just drove past me as if I were not there. At that time, I wished that I really wasn't there. The man I had loved for so many years had cheated on me. If it hadn't been for my daughters, I would have thrown myself in front of one of those cars that was driving past me. When I think about it now, it is ironic that what he created with me saved my life. I don't know what time I reached the hotel, but I went straight to bed and surprisingly slept quite well. Perhaps all the crying had made me tired. Luckily the girls were staying at their uncle's house and didn't see me when I was crying. My husband didn't come back to the room that night. The next day we returned home but did not talk to each other in the car. The girls could sense that there was something wrong. We told them that we had been drinking too much at the wedding and had hangovers. My husband had met that woman on a business trip and had been having an affair with her for a few months. She was from another town so when my husband went away on business, they would spend some time together. When the wedding came along, he booked her a hotel not far from where we would be staying. He didn't know that some of the guests would be staying there, so he thought that there would be no way for me to find him. I am sure he hadn't planned to spend the whole night with her, but he knew that he could not return to me that night. He apologised to me, but I wouldn't have him back. He rented a small place where he lived alone. That woman was married but her husband was an alcoholic and only cared about the bottle. She spent more and more time with my husband until he was diagnosed with cancer. When he needed to be looked after she disappeared from his life, and I was left to care for him at our home until he had to move into a special home where he died. It all happened quite quickly. Marit has never accepted his death. Please don't let her know that I told you about it."

When Tom walked into the living room, he could hear that Marit was up, and knew he wouldn't have to wait much longer for breakfast. They had brown cheese, which Marit explained was goat's cheese, on bread and some milk. After breakfast, Marit took Tom to the lake where they sat on a big rock and spoke about life in their respective countries. Marit had never been to England but said that she had watched a lot of English television. For Tom, it was hard to imagine how different summer life and winter life could be. As they were sitting on the rock looking at the calm lake, they heard a car and when they went back to the house Hilde and her boyfriend Erik had arrived. Marit said that after lunch they would be going to her flat in Tromso for a few days. Hilde was helping her mother in the kitchen while Erik was on the veranda rolling cigarettes and Astrid was reading a magazine after her lie-in. Tom went to his room to pack his things, but when Marit saw what he was doing she said that there would not be enough room in the car, so he should only take the essential things like his toothbrush. Marit's mother had prepared salmon for lunch, served with potatoes. Tom enjoyed the meal, but there was a bit too much Norwegian being spoken for his liking as it made him feel left out. Having had a late Sunday-lunch, it was evening when Tom got into the car with Erik and the two girls, leaving Astrid and her mother behind. Erik put some heavy-metal music on and listened to all the tracks excitedly before switching to the much calmer radio station, which was a relief to his passengers. The drive wasn't too long and soon they reached a small town where they slowed down and parked outside a small block of flats. They took up some bags and Marit opened the door for them to enter her flat. It was a small studio flat with a corridor for hanging coats, a toilet straight ahead and the main room that served as a living room, kitchen and bedroom. There was no table, just a work surface in the small kitchen, so they sat on a rug in the middle of the room having taken a cushion each from the bed for extra comfort. The conversation flowed almost as freely as the wine, but unfortunately for Tom, they were both Norwegian. Tom had a glass, but he was not a great wine-drinker and certainly did not favour wine without food. Hilde said she was allergic to wine, and Erik abstained from drinking as he would be driving, but Marit didn't hold back and seemed to enjoy the next glass even more than the preceding one. Several bottles later, Marit staggered off to the bathroom and while she was still there Erik and Hilde got up to leave. Tom was not happy to be left alone with the drunken Marit who was refusing to leave the bathroom, so Hilde agreed to talk to her and after a good ten minutes managed to persuade her to unlock the door. With Marit ready to leave the bathroom Hilde and Erik wasted no time in calling it a night and embarking on the drive back home. Marit was expressing her dislike for life and her red hair in no uncertain terms, stating that redheads were witches and should be burned. She then offered herself to Tom sexually, but Tom was more interested in calming things down, and though he did not find her unattractive under normal circumstances, felt it would be wrong to pursue intimacy of a sexual nature at that moment as she was clearly under the influence of alcohol; besides, he didn't want her to throw up on him in the middle of lovemaking. Marit did not want to take no for an answer and told Tom that there was only one bed and that she would force her way upon him, but Tom noticed a mattress on the floor under the bed and pulled it out to make himself a bed for the night. Marit accepted defeat and told Tom that she would sleep on the mattress promising to leave Tom alone in her bed. He needn't have worried, as she was fast asleep almost before her head hit the pillow.

Day 15 Monday

First thing the next morning, Marit told Tom that because of what had happened the night before, he was no longer welcome there. She said that there was a bus leaving for Narvik, passing her hometown, where Erik would be waiting to put his haversack on the bus. When Tom said that he didn't have cash for the ticket, as an excuse not to leave, she gave him some money for his fare emphasising that it was just a loan and told him how to get to the bus station. Tom took the money with no intention of returning it, as he was angry at the way she had reacted to his gentlemanly conduct. He left wondering how things could have been different had he gone with the flow of her alcohol-driven desire.

The bus station wasn't difficult to find, and the bus began its four-hour journey on time. As the bus approached Marit's village, Tom scanned the immediate landscape, but there was no sign of Erik. A woman with red hair, accompanied by two small children and an elderly man, were standing by the roadside at the bus stop. Tom knew that the bus that had been making mostly request stops would be stopping, and after the woman and children had said goodbye to the elderly man and paid the driver, Tom asked the driver how far the next stop would be, hoping to buy enough time for Erik to arrive. The driver mentioned the name of the next stop and pushed the button for the doors to close. Tom squeezed through the closing door with agility. He knew that he could not continue his journey without his haversack that contained all his belongings apart from his toothbrush which he had taken with him in a small paper bag. As the bus left, Tom immediately began to regret not having explained the situation to the bus driver who may have understood the seriousness of the matter and waited a few minutes. Tom's regret increased to the level of self-kicking when a white car driven by Erik appeared with the bus still in view. Perhaps they could still chase the bus and Tom could continue his journey to Narvik, but Erik stopped the car, laid Tom's haversack by the side of the road, and drove off without a word. "Marit must have made up a pretty damning story for Erik to behave in such an unfriendly manner," Tom thought. He checked the secret knot on the haversack to make sure it had not been opened. Everything was as he had left it, and he was pleased to find Solveig's apple pie he had forgotten about, as he had not eaten that day.

It was a beautiful day with not a cloud in the sky, so after finishing his apple pie, Tom began to walk in the direction of Narvik, enjoying the sunshine and clean air knowing full well that he could not reach his destination on foot. With very few vehicles passing, Tom thought it could be difficult to hitch a ride, so despite enjoying the fresh air, he began to raise his thumb every time he heard a car. To his surprise, the third car that passed him stopped and reversed to offer him a lift. When Tom said that he wanted to go to Narvik, the driver, who was a middle-aged man with a goatee and long mousy hair that was going grey, said that it would probably take him several lifts to get that far but offered to take him all the way if he could wait until after lunch as he had some business to attend to at home. Tom said that he was in no hurry and the man who said that his name was Karl told Tom to put his haversack on the back seat of the car next to the shopping. Karl asked Tom what he was doing so far from home and how he liked it in one of the most northern places in the world. It was not long before they turned into a dirt road and drove until they reached a large wooden house. Karl gathered the shopping and told Tom that he could leave his things in the car, but Tom said that he might need something and took his haversack with him. As they entered the house, Karl shouted something in Norwegian but then almost mid-sentence switched to English and said that they had a visitor from England. A woman with long brown hair came towards them, said that she was Eva and shook hands with Tom welcoming him to that part of the world. Karl explained to Eva that Tom was on his way to Narvik and would be staying for lunch. He then uttered something in Norwegian followed by a muffled chuckle as he put the shopping on the kitchen table. Karl poured himself some coffee that Eva had prepared, saying that he could not live without it. He pointed to the coffee pot and told Tom to help himself. Eva and Tom followed Karl into the living room where Tom sat in a light green armchair with floral cloths on the armrests.

Karl looked at him and said, "The last person who sat there was murdered." Eva looked at Karl with a slightly tilted head and tightened lips as if to ask him not to say anything.

But he continued, "He was a hitchhiker just like you. It was late summer. I was driving back from a meeting in another town when I stopped for a coffee. I bought a newspaper and sat down to drink my coffee when a young man with rusty brown hair and a short beard asked me in English if he could borrow my newspaper to see if they were showing a certain football match on television that afternoon. I knew that they were going to show the match, so I pointed it out to him in my paper and before I knew it, we were discussing matters related to football. He told me that his name was George and that he had been hitch-hiking from his native Romania and wanted to get as far north as possible without using public transport. He said that he had been walking for several hours up to that point, unable to hitch a ride, so when I finished my coffee, I offered to give him a lift which he gladly accepted. I told him that I would drop him off just before my destination from where he could get a lift, but as we got closer to my home, I thought it might be nice to watch the match together as I knew that my wife would be out until after the match. When I suggested that he could come to my house to watch the match and that I could take him to the main road to get a lift after the match, he seemed very relieved and thanked me. Eva was getting into her car to drive to her yoga class when we arrived at the house. I'd been away for a day, so she was happy to see me but seemed surprised that I had a guest with me. I told George that he could leave his rucksack in the car, but like you he said that he might need something and brought it in with him. There was some food and snacks in the kitchen. All that was missing was beer. George sat in the armchair where you are sitting right now, and when I suggested that we could drive to town and get some beer, he said that he was very tired and asked if he could stay there and take a nap instead. Even though he was a stranger, I decided I could trust him alone in my house as we were in the middle of nowhere and I wouldn't be gone for long. On the way back from buying the beers my car had a mechanical problem. But luckily, I got help and despite a short delay was away for no more than 40 minutes. When I passed the living room on the way to the kitchen, George seemed to be asleep in the armchair. I took two beers and put the rest in the fridge to cool for later. The match was about to kick off, so I put the beers on the table in the living room and took the remote control as I glanced at George, but I suddenly froze. He had been shot in the chest. I immediately called the police who confirmed that he was dead and began looking for clues and asking questions. All I could tell them was that his name was George and he was from Romania. I hadn't even asked him what town he was from. The police said that as there were no signs of any struggle, and that he must have opened the door to the murderer in a planned burglary but then changed his mind because I had been kind to him. But they couldn't understand why he had been shot sitting down. I told them that I usually left the door unlocked when there was someone at home and suggested that as he was very tired when I left, he may have been shot in his sleep. Nothing had been taken from our house, but his rucksack had gone and even his wristwatch was missing. A few days later, the police told me that his pockets had been completely emptied, which they thought meant that his identity would have linked him to his murderer and surmised that the murderer was probably from Romania and would have already left the country. They sent the body to Romania and transferred the case with all the information they had to the Romanian police. The image of the corpse in my living room haunted me. And for several weeks I felt uncomfortable leaving Eva alone in the house, though I was sure lightning would not strike twice. Gradually normality resumed in our lives and I once again began to go on the occasional business trip. One evening I was dining at a restaurant in Oslo where I had been attending a weekend seminar. It was a particularly cold evening and I was enjoying a warm meal when a man, who had clearly been drinking more than he could handle, began to become rowdy as he was preparing to leave. The young blond man appeared to be leaving against his will; and as he left, he complained that the drinks were too weak, which was ironic. Having noticed that I had become distracted and stopped eating, the waiter calmly apologised for the noise and asked if he could get me anything. It took me a while before I could continue eating. Something about the young man disturbed me. That night I fell asleep with his voice still echoing in my head. I woke up in the middle of the night with the voice still ringing in my head, and as I lay in the dark still half asleep with no distractions, I suddenly got a flashback from George. Apart from the accent, the voice from the restaurant belonged to George. It was as if the murdered Romanian had been reincarnated as a beardless Norwegian with blond hair. The thought of it sent shivers down my spine. After much deliberation, I decided to go to the police and tell them what had happened. They thanked me but didn't seem very interested. A week or so later, I was at home one evening reading a newspaper when there was a knock on my door. It was a detective from the police department who thanked me for the information I had given them and said that they had solved the case and made several arrests. He told me that the person I knew as George was actually a Norwegian criminal who together with an accomplice planned to murder a rival gang leader. Having a similar build to the victim, he grew a beard, dyed his hair and dressed himself up to be indistinguishable from him to the unsuspecting eye of a stranger. They had kidnapped the victim and shot him in the chest. When I went to town to buy beer, the man who called himself George let his friend in, and they put the body where you are sitting now. Obviously, when I got back and discovered the dead body, I assumed it belonged to the Romanian hitchhiker I had picked up. Being a respected member of society, there was no reason for the police not to believe my statement and they were happy to send the body to Romania. The criminals had done all this so that the police would get rid of the body for them and close the case in Norway."

Tom thought deeply for a while and then asked, "Where was the man killed? If he was killed in Oslo, it would probably have taken almost a day to drive here, and the time of death would have been different. How did they know you would stop for coffee and what would they have done if you had not given him a lift and left him alone in your home? And why were the police not looking for someone fitting his descriptions if he had been reported kidnapped or missing?"

Karl smiled and replied, "They must have sedated him and shot him where the body was found. The police did not carry out an autopsy as the cause of death was obvious. The criminals had probably been following me and waiting for me to stop for coffee which I was bound to do as it was a very long drive. They may have known my habits. If I had not left him alone in the house, he would have probably left later, and the body would have been found near my house for me to identify as the Romanian hitchhiker. I suppose if their plans had gone wrong, they could have dumped the body in the lake that would have soon been frozen over for the winter. The police would most probably have been looking for a missing person, but the criminals took a chance and successfully deceived them. These are all very good questions, but the truth is that none of this really happened. I am writing a novel and wanted to see how you would react to the story. I will consider your questions to make the story more watertight." Tom thought about sharing his ambition of becoming a novelist with Karl but decided against it.

While Karl was getting some work done, Tom spent some time in the garden with Eva who was picking vegetables for lunch, but he was in deep thought. The story had made him realise how much imagination he would need to come up with something to write about.

After lunch, Karl drove Tom to Narvik. The drive took much less than it would have by bus and before long Tom was being dropped off at train station, which was a short walk from the bus station where he would have got off the bus. Erik's tardiness had worked in Tom's favour.

There was a train leaving that evening arriving in Stockholm the following night with three changes including an overnight stay in Kiruna, but Tom thought it would be better to spend the night in Narvik and take a direct train the next morning. Or perhaps there was a better way of getting to Stockholm. The station was small and there was not much activity at the time, but Tom noticed a bearded tourist with a large haversack sitting on a platform bench and went over to ask if he was going to Stockholm. The man told Tom in an Australian accent that he had missed the morning train and would, therefore, be taking the evening train, as he didn't want to spend another night in Narvik. He said that his name was Richard and that he had been away from his native Australia for three months with another three months to go.

"How come you missed your train?" asked Tom.

"Well, I was sitting on a bench in town yesterday afternoon when a woman in her late 30s early 40s came and sat next to me. She started talking about Jesus, but when I told her that I wasn't interested in religion she said that she respected that and wouldn't try to convert me. She said that her son had become very ill when he was a baby, and the doctors had given him very little chance of surviving. She asked God for his help and suddenly he made a full recovery. The doctors said it was a miracle. Since then, she had been spreading the word of God. We talked about a lot of other things and when I said that I was going to sleep at the station she said that she didn't live far from there and I could spend the night on her couch if I wanted. Her name was Karen, and she had quite a nice flat with a big leather couch. I met her 13-year-old son, who left his PlayStation for a few minutes to meet me. We played a few games while she was getting food ready, but I spent most of the evening in the kitchen eating a bit and talking a lot; well, she did most of the talking. It was all going well until a neighbour knocked on the door. She was only there for a few minutes and I don't know what she wanted because I didn't understand the language, but when she left Karen told me that I couldn't spend the night there because the neighbour had seen me and if she saw me leaving in the morning she would think that we were lovers and gossip about it. She made a few phone calls and then told me that a DJ who was a bachelor would put me up for the night. About 10 minutes later we heard a car hooting and when we looked out of the window Karen confirmed that it was the DJ Rolf. I went down to the car, told him that my name was Richard, put my rucksack on the backseat and we drove off. Rolf didn't say a word. It felt a bit awkward, but when we walked into his house his mood changed. He became friendly and jovial. He grabbed a can of beer from the fridge and tossed it over to me, which luckily, I caught. His house was small and very untidy. There was unwashed crockery in the sink and his coffee table in the sitting room was covered with opened letters and newspapers leaving just enough room for some empty beer cans and an ashtray. There were even papers on the couch. He pushed the papers on the table together to make a neater pile and took the papers from the couch to make room for me, placing them on top of the pile on the table. He then took the empty beer cans to the kitchen and came back with a six-pack putting on some loud music and

101

lighting a rolled-up cigarette before sitting down. He was a skinny guy with a blond beard and had a tattoo of an angel on his left arm, which I thought conveyed a message of love, but he had the letters R-O-L-F tattooed on the knuckles of his right fist, making him look like a fighter. We talked and drank a lot of beer until moving on to the hard stuff. The next thing I remember I woke up with a headache, looked at my watch and realised that I was going to miss my train if I didn't hurry up. The house was quiet; I looked in his bedroom; his bed was unmade, but Rolf wasn't there. I wrote him a note to thank him and tell him that I was on my way to the station to catch the 11:38 train, hoping that he might catch up with me and drive me to the station. I took my stuff and hurried out of the front door with my head pounding from all the drinks I had downed the night before. I knew the direction but wasn't sure of the quickest way to get to the station, so I walked as fast as I could and asked locals the way without stopping. When I reached the station, the train was there, but it had already started to move and all I could do was watch it gather speed leaving me behind. I don't want to spend another 24 hours here so I will take the train this evening."

Tom wanted to go to town, but Richard said that although he still had several hours to wait, he would rather stay at the station and take it easy. After asking Richard for directions to the shopping mall, Tom left alone, but was soon caught up by two girls who had overheard him getting directions and asked if they could follow him. They said they were Margaret and Agnes from Poland on their way to Stockholm but had run out of food and needed to buy some for their trip. The shopping centre was not far from the station and easy to find. After their shopping, the girls wanted to go back and wait for their train. Tom told them that he would be taking the direct train the following morning. The two girls conferred in Polish and then asked Tom where he would be sleeping that night, telling him that they thought accommodation was too expensive in Norway. Tom said that he didn't have anywhere in mind and was happy to sleep at the station. The girls said that they had been discussing which train to take and had decided that they would take the morning train if they could hang out with Tom and perhaps also some other tourists who would be taking the same train. Having decided that they were in no hurry to get back to the station they walked in the opposite direction looking for a nice place to eat some of the food they had just bought. It was a sunny day and they soon found a nice patch of grass where they sat to eat, sharing each other's food for variety. Tom couldn't fail to notice that Margaret's blond plaited hair was long enough for her to sit on. She was wearing a white t-shirt, a denim skirt just about covering her knees and a pair of sandals, while Agnes with her average-length wavy brown hair was wearing a light blue t-shirt and jeans with trainers. When they had finished eating, they tidied up and Agnes went in search of a bin to throw the empty paper bags away. Tom and Margaret sat there talking, waiting for her to return, but after 15 minutes began to worry that perhaps something was wrong. Just as Tom was about to go and look for her, she appeared coming down the hill. She had met an elderly couple who were sitting eating sandwiches on a bench near the bin where she had disposed of the rubbish. They had seen her picnicking with Tom and Margaret and were wondering where they had come from and what they were doing in Narvik. When Agnes told them that they were planning to sleep at the station or maybe pitch a tent that night, they said that they could camp in their garden for one night. Agnes had returned to discuss the matter with Margaret and Tom, and was happy to learn that Tom too had a tent with him. She took them to the bench where the elderly couple were sitting, to say that they would like to accept their invitation. The old man who was rather tall for his generation said, "We saw you eating over there on the grass. It's our wedding anniversary today and we like to celebrate it every year here on this bench because this is where we met for the first time." His wife continued, "We used to go out to eat on our anniversary, and we still do if the weather isn't good, but coming here is more special." The couple were friendly and spoke very good English. Einar said that he had worked as a pilot while his wife Nora had been a housewife busy bringing up their two children.

He said, "Luckily, I didn't have to spend much time away from home as I was flying a small aircraft taking tourists to various parts of Lapland. This is why I speak English. I used to spend a lot of time with the passengers once we had landed because they had usually booked a round trip and were happy to spend time with a native who knew the geography and history of the area, even though we always had an official guide with us. When the children got a bit older Nora got a job at the tourist office here in Narvik."

While he was talking, they reached a red wooden house, and he unlatched the gate door inviting them all into the garden. Tom looked around to find the best spot for his tent. Margaret and Agnes were also looking around and they all seemed to be drawn to the space under an apple tree. They had just put their things down and were planning where exactly to lay their tents out when they heard a woman call as she opened the gate. Nora rushed to her and greeted her with a hug and kiss. Einar greeted the woman, who was thin with long brown hair and carrying a large bag, in a similar fashion. They were so involved in conversation that they went into the house without a word to the campers in their garden, but moments later as Tom and the girls were beginning to open their haversacks to remove their tents Nora came out to the garden and said, "That was our daughter; she has baked us some cake. Would you like to come in and celebrate our anniversary with us? You can bring your things into the house and put your tents up later. It doesn't get dark here." Nora showed her guests into the house. There was a very small room immediately as they entered for leaving shoes, umbrellas and outdoor jackets followed by another door leading to the living area.

As they walked in Nora introduced the woman by saying, "This is my daughter Karen. She has surprised us by bringing us a delicious home-baked cake on our anniversary."

Karen said, "It was God's will that they should meet, and I thank Jesus every day for that and for my existence."

Tom thought it was a bit odd but smiled and nodded his head. Soon Karen had moved on to Margaret and Agnes asking them if they had found Jesus. Tom could see that they were not comfortable with that subject. Suddenly he remembered the religious woman whom Richard had met was called Karen, so when she continued preaching and said to them all, "It was God's will that you would meet my parents and come here for me to give you his message," Tom said, "My powers tell me that there is a bearded man in your life."

"Yes, it is Jesus," replied Karen.

"No," said Tom, "It is not Jesus. It is a man from afar. Well, he is not in your life but could have been a source of embarrassment if you had not acted quickly and sent him to the land of music."

By this time the room was silent as Karen recognised the story and stood there in amazement.

Tom continued, "You have a son you nearly lost many years ago. It is a miracle that he is alive. He may be distant from you at times, but I can tell you that he loves you very much."

Einar and Nora were astonished to hear a complete stranger talk about their grandson like that, and Karen, who had a tear in her eye, could tell by their expressions that they had not told Tom anything. Tom realised that he had gone too far and was feeling guilty, but there was no turning back, so he continued, "There is a lot of love in this family. I wish you all the best." The family smiled and the Polish girls looked at their new friend in admiration. Karen was there for another two hours and did not once mention religion again. They had the carrot cake that Karen had baked and coffee while discussing various subjects such as education in their respective countries, the royal family and mosquitoes in Lapland. After Karen had left, Tom suggested that they should go to the garden and put their tents up, but Nora said that unless they really wanted to sleep in the garden, they could use the two spare rooms they had. She put some bread and goat's cheese on the table with a few slices of cake that remained from earlier, and after Tom, Margaret and Agnes had had enough to eat they were shown to their rooms. Tom reminded everyone of the train's departure time and bid them all goodnight before going into his room and closing the curtains on another day.

Day 16 Tuesday

It was another sunny day when Tom woke up and opened the window. There was still plenty of time to get ready and go to the station. Einar was in the garden and Nora could be heard pottering about in the kitchen. Meanwhile, Margaret and Agnes were still asleep, so Tom went straight to the bathroom to avoid any queues. There were three clean towels folded on top of a laundry basket, so Tom showered and used one of the towels. When he had finished in the bathroom, he opened the door and could hear the girls speaking Polish in the other room. As soon as he went to his room, one of the girls went into the bathroom. After getting ready Tom went to the kitchen where he greeted Nora and Einar who had just walked in from the garden. Breakfast was already on the table, but the couple said that they had been up since seven o'clock and already eaten. Tom sat at the table and was helping himself to dark bread and a variety of toppings when Margaret and Agnes walked into the kitchen and greeted everyone collectively with a good morning and a smile, looking fresh after their long sleep and showers. They joined Tom for breakfast and exchanged pleasantries with their hosts.

During breakfast, Agnes turned to Nora and said, "Yesterday your husband mentioned that while he was working as a pilot, you were bringing up two children; we met Karen yesterday, but what happened to your other child?"

Nora smiled and said, "Thomas was a keen skier. I remember when he was 19 one winter and studying at Oslo University, he came home for his winter break as usual. He used to go skiing every day when he was here. One day he didn't come back at the usual time. After almost two hours Einar and I started to worry that perhaps something bad had happened. The sound of an ambulance in the distance increased our anxiety to an unbearable level, so we decided to go out and see if we could find him. Suddenly, we heard the creaking of the gate, followed by footsteps in the garden. We opened the door and saw Thomas walking towards us. He said that he had been talking to someone over coffee and had not noticed the passing of the time. The same thing happened the next day; this time we were not worried, just a bit curious. On the third day, he didn't even take his skis with him. We noticed when he had already left, so we couldn't ask him where he was going. We just had to hope that everything was OK. We had noticed that he had been acting strangely and was in his own thoughts, but when we questioned him, he denied that there was anything wrong. That evening he came back earlier, but this time he had a girl with him. He had met Lucy while skiing and they had fallen in love instantly. She was from Canada, and a few months later Thomas moved to Toronto where he finished his education and is now living with his wife Lucy and their two boys. We visit them every year either for Christmas or in the summer. Next month they are coming here for the first time as a family."

Straight after breakfast, before Nora could stop her, Margaret washed the dishes, and the three visitors thanked their hosts as they gathered their belongings in preparation to leave. On the way to the station, Margaret and Agnes told Tom how impressed they were with his psychic powers and asked if he could tell what lay ahead for them. Tom admitted that he did not possess any psychic powers and told them about the Australian he had met at the station.

Margaret laughed and said, "Back in Poland two of my friends were at a cafeteria drinking coffee together when a Gypsy woman walked in and asked them for money. They said that they were students and didn't have any money to spare. The woman said that she would tell their fortune if they paid her, but they insisted that they didn't have money and were not interested. The woman looked at them scornfully, pointed at them with a wagging finger and said threateningly, "I will curse you. Within three years, you two will be married, and your first child will be a son who will be born hideously deformed." She then turned around and walked out of the coffee shop leaving everyone with hairs standing on their backs, except for my two friends who were laughing, as they were brother and sister."

There was still food left from the previous day's shopping, but they popped into a shop and added a few more items to their food supply. When they arrived at the station, the train was already there, with plenty of time before departure. Tom suggested that they board the train to find good seats. They chose their seats knowing that they would be spending the rest of the day and the whole night there. Most of the passengers on the train seemed to be young backpackers just like Tom, which made him feel that he was in the right place. The train was soon in Sweden, but there was still a long way before they would reach their destination of Stockholm. Every time the train stopped at small stations Tom would look out of the window and wonder why anyone would choose to live there and how they would avoid dying of boredom. The occasional tourist would get on the train, which would intrigue Tom as to how they had even found such a remote place. It wasn't until late afternoon that Tom and the girls took down their bags to take out some of the food they knew would have to last them until the next morning. After eating, while putting the rest of the food away, Tom remembered that he had a pack of cards that Kristian had given him, so he asked if Margaret and Agnes would like to play. The girls thought it was a great idea as they had so much time to kill. Tom suggested a few games, but the girls didn't know them, so when Agnes named a game that Margaret knew and said that it was easy to learn they all seemed happy. After a few games, Tom had got the hang of it and was winning his share of the games.

The train had just left one of the many small stations when a man short in stature with greyish hair and a moustache to match stood above them and in an English accent asked, "Are you professional gamblers?"

"No," replied Tom, looking a bit surprised.

"I didn't think so," the man retorted. "I can usually tell. I can spot them from a mile away, you know." He then tossed his green rucksack onto the overhead rack and said, "D'you mind if I do?" while grabbing the seat next to Tom without waiting for an answer. "My name's Robert," he said, tapping the side of his nose and looking at Tom. "Don't tell anyone and you'll be OK. What's your name, rank and date of birth?" Tom told him his name but ignored the other questions. "Who are these delicious young fillies?" he asked looking at Margaret and Agnes. "You're not married to them, are you? I wouldn't want to be stepping on any toes," he said with a wink.

"This is my wife Margaret," said Tom. "We are on our honeymoon and this is sister Agnes, the priest who married us. We bumped into her in Lapland. We were very hungry and she turned our bread into sandwiches. It was a miracle."

"Do you take me for a fool?" said Robert, moving slightly closer to Tom and looking at him suspiciously. "You're not wearing wedding rings. I can spot these things from a mile you know. I've been trained to spot wedding rings. When I first walked onto this train, I said to myself, "Those people aren't wearing wedding rings; either they're not married, or they've lost their wedding rings gambling."

"That's amazing," said Tom. "We lost our wedding rings to a reindeer herder in a game of poker up in Lapland."

"Yes," added Margaret, "Our wedding rings and two sausages. That's why we only had bread to eat when we met sister Agnes."

Robert took a deep breath through his nose, held his head up and puffed his chest out with pride, "Years of training. Years of training. Never wrong."

Tom looked at Margaret with a secretive smile. He was glad to see that Margaret, who had not protested when he had told Robert that they were married, was truly on his side and had a similar sense of humour to his. The conductor came to check the tickets of all new passengers who had just got on. Robert looked at him tapping the side of his nose twice, and the conductor walked on.

"Don't have to pay; they know who I am. They feel safer when I'm on one of their trains. I could fly to Rio tomorrow and not pay a penny."

"Why do you need to know about wedding rings?" asked Agnes.

"If I'm interrogating someone, I can put more pressure on him if I know he's a family man. I lean on them until they crack. A man with a ring will cry under pressure."

"Are you going to Stockholm?" asked Tom.

"It's all pretty hush hush," answered Robert tapping the side of this nose again. "If I tell you, soon the whole train will know, and my cover will be blown. No, I will just disappear into the dark." And at the next stop, he did. The train had been at the station for about two minutes when, as if he had suddenly realised where he was, he grabbed his bag and said, "Duty calls, cheerio," and was gone. Less than a minute later the train pulled out of the station and the Polish girls looked at each other and laughed. The abandoned game of cards was only played until the end of that particular hand in an attempt to get back to normality and then put away so as not to attract any other strange characters. Margaret and Agnes sat planning their trip back to Poland. They said that they had already been to Stockholm on a previous trip and liked it there, but wanted to go straight back to Poland this time. They had travelled up through the Baltic countries and Finland to Lapland and wanted to return to Poland through Sweden, Denmark and Germany. Tom told them that after Stockholm he wanted to visit Finland, so they told him where they had been and what they recommended. It was getting late and Tom knew that he needed to get some sleep, so he decided to stretch his legs by taking a walk down the train and brushing his teeth on the way back. Some of the other passengers were already sleeping; others were talking and some reading, but when he walked into the third carriage from his own, he was struck by a voice he recognised. It was Robert, talking to a tourist, telling him something about martial arts and how he could disarm a man and kill him with his own weapon. Tom was astonished to see Robert still on the train and although he was sitting with his back to him, he quickly turned around and walked back to where Margaret and Agnes were sitting to tell them whom he had just seen. He was in such a hurry he forgot to brush his teeth and as the girls were already waiting to do their teeth, he let them go before him. Tom, Margaret and Agnes made themselves as comfortable as they possibly could for a night's sleep on the train and were only mildly disturbed by the train stopping at stations and the sound of cheerful reunions and chatter on the platform, until at one of the stops the train seemed to stay for much longer, and as Tom was about to drift back to sleep the noise on the platform became unmistakably different and much louder. Tom and the girls looked out of the window to see Robert handcuffed and being led away by two large armed policemen. Shortly after the train had begun to move again, two police officers walked into the carriage, one holding a picture, and said something in Swedish before asking in English if anyone had spoken with the person in the picture. Tom was not surprised to see that it was a picture of Robert and raised his hand to draw the attention of the police officers. The policewoman was of average height with blond hair and the policeman was quite a bit taller. They were both friendly and spoke quite good English, asking Tom and the girls what Robert had been doing and telling them. After Tom had told them the whole story they smiled and said that they may have been saved by their sense of humour and inventiveness, as Robert was targeting tourists to steal from them and even try to befriend and recruit vulnerable young men to his world of crime and perversion.

The police officer said, "By telling him that you had lost even your last sausage in gambling he probably thought you were not worth robbing and as you pretended to be a married man he just moved on. A plain-clothes police officer noticed him moving from one car to the other talking to tourists and eyeing their belongings. We were alerted when he was caught in the act. We are very happy that he has been captured. Stealing is one of his lesser crimes." The officers then moved on to talk with other witnesses to see if they had lost anything. When the train reached Stockholm in the morning, Tom saw them get off the train looking satisfied with the information they had gathered.

Day 17 Wednesday

As Margaret and Agnes had already been to Stockholm, Tom was hoping that they would show him around a bit, but they said that they only had three hours before their next train. They decided to spend that time close to the station and have something to eat. Tom bought a packet of cinnamon buns and the girls who would be travelling by train again bought considerably more food for their journey. They went to a nearby park and sat on a bench near a fountain to eat their breakfast. It seemed to be a popular place for people to take it easy and watch other people go by. Margaret and Agnes took the opportunity to give their addresses to Tom and said that he could visit them when he passes through Poland. It was then time for them to head back to the station and find the train to Copenhagen. The girls said that they had enjoyed their adventures and thanked Tom for helping them. Agnes gave Tom a goodbye hug and got on the train, but to Tom's surprise Margaret's hug turned into a kiss.

"Well, we are married," she said with a cheeky smile as she turned around and got on the train. By then Agnes had found them a seat and Tom stood below their window as they waved goodbye. Tom waved to them both, but he could really only see Margaret.

As Tom passed the lockers, he contemplated leaving his luggage there to give him more freedom to wander about town but decided that the money would be better spent on food, and having his luggage with him would mean that he wouldn't have to go back to the station to pick it up. Tom was alone again, and he began to walk rather aimlessly following other tourists until he came to what looked like the old part of town. There were narrow cobbled streets with small shops hoping to sell highly priced items to elderly American tourists. Tom walked through the old town until he came to the modern part of Stockholm and crossed a bridge where he found some museums and some benches facing the sea. He sat for a while watching the boats go by and began to think about his upcoming trip to Finland. He wanted to see as much of Stockholm as possible but it was so peaceful sitting there under the warm sun, that was cooled sufficiently by the sea breeze, that he decided to lean against his haversack, which he had laid on the bench beside him, and rest for a while. He soon dozed off and when he awoke, dark clouds were gathering and he felt a chill in the air, so he rose quickly to his feet, picked up his haversack and began walking rapidly towards the bridge, knowing that he would have to cross the bridge to find Pia's house as he had been on a small island. He was told that it was two miles away and was recommended to take a bus. Knowing that he could manage two miles, he set off in the direction of Pia's house, getting confirmation every 10 minutes or so that he was still heading in the right direction, but being told that he should really take a bus. He had estimated he should be able to cover that distance in 45 minutes to an hour on foot, but after an hour of walking he felt that he was no closer than when he had started, as he was still being advised to go by bus. He was no longer in the centre of town, but he was being reassured that he was going in the right direction, which seemed to be taking forever without getting any closer as he was still hearing that he was about two miles away. Eventually, he asked a dark-haired man who told him that he was about 15 kilometres from his destination. Tom was sure that the man was mistaken but the man said that a Swedish mile was not the same as an English mile. The man who was

116

standing outside his house said without hesitation, "Come, I'll give you a lift." As he drove, he told Tom that he was Amir from Iran and had been living in Sweden for eight years.

"When I first came to Sweden, I didn't speak any Swedish and knew very little English. My brother Rostam was already in Sweden, but he moved to America after a year. By that time, I had been to a course to learn Swedish and had some friends. I studied to become a dentist and had to learn English for that too. I work as a dentist at a hospital in Stockholm but my main passion is photography. My wife is from Finland. She works as a nurse at the same hospital as me. We have two small children." Suddenly he slammed his foot on the brakes, "Oh God, I left the children alone at home. I must go back." He then put his hands on his forehead for a second before breathing out a sigh of relief and saying, "No, it's OK; I just remembered. My mother-in-law is with them." and drove on. He apologised for the confusion saying, "I have a lot to think about. I would like to quit my job and open a photography shop, but I'm not sure I will be successful. Also, I miss my family back home. My grandparents are very old, and I am afraid I might never see them again. But I don't want to bother you with my problems."

He then stopped and looked at the house number on the paper, got out of the car, opened the backdoor and gave Tom his haversack before shaking hands and wishing the grateful Tom a nice stay. As Tom rang the doorbell a few drops of rain began to fall and he wished that Amir had waited to make sure there was somebody at home. It was a white brick house with high windows and quite a large garden. Moments later, Pia opened the door and took Tom up to meet her mother: a stylish woman with hair straight out of a hairdresser's catalogue and long red nails.

Her mother greeted Tom and then had a short conversation with Pia before turning to Tom and saying, "I'm sorry but you can't stay here tonight. Pia's father is away on business and I don't want a strange man in my house."

She had barely finished her sentence when the lights went out. Pia said that she would go and get some candles, but her mother began to panic, "My favourite TV programme is starting in five minutes. I can't miss it. I never miss it. What am I going to do?"

Tom noticed that the neighbours across the road had their lights on and thought it was probably a fuse. He asked where the fuse box was, but neither Pia nor her mother understood that word, so Tom described it and said that it was probably near the front door. Pia's mother said that there was a white box on the wall behind the house that fitted the descriptions Tom had given. Tom found the box on the wall behind the house and switched the main fuse back on. Both Pia and her mother were impressed. Pia's mother was delighted that she would be able to watch her favourite programme and thanked Tom, telling him that he would be welcome to spend the night there. Pia took Tom to her room while her mother sat glued to the television watching the programme so dear to her. Pia told Tom that she and her friend Ulrika had both been compensated by their insurance companies and as she had spent much less money without her credit card during her trip, they both had enough money to take another trip the following month. Pia's mother was happy watching television and Tom didn't see her until the next morning.

Day 18 Thursday

The next morning, Tom woke up later than he had recently, enjoying a few more hours of darkness than he had up north. He had fully recovered from his night on the train, where he had managed only a few hours of uninterrupted sleep. As he walked from the bedroom into the living room, he was greeted by Pia's mother and the smell of bacon. She thought, being English, he would appreciate egg and bacon for breakfast, which he did. She also asked him if he had any dirty laundry, as she was about to put in a load. Tom said that he was leaving that day, but he was reassured that they had a dryer and that the entire process would take no more than two hours. After a hearty breakfast, Pia took Tom into the garden where they sat on the garden swing. It had been raining, but now there was more blue sky than clouds, with no threat of rain. Tom had decided to take the ferry to Turku in Finland that evening and asked Pia if she had ever been there.

"No, I haven't been to Turku, but I have been to Helsinki," she said. "I went with a bunch of friends to party on the ship. We didn't even get off at Helsinki harbour."

Tom liked to party but couldn't imagine not wanting to get off and see a new place. It was nearing noon when Pia's mother came out into the garden and announced that she was going into town and could give Pia and Tom a lift. When Tom went into the house, Pia's mother handed him his clean laundry, still warm and smelling fresh, for him to pack into his haversack. Tom and Pia went to the car and waited for her mother to lock up and drive them to town. They were dropped off near the park where Tom had eaten his breakfast the previous day, and waited a few minutes for Ulrika, whom Pia had arranged to meet. She was a plump girl with short brown hair and glasses.

The first thing she said was, "Let's go and have something to eat."

Tom wasn't surprised to hear that coming from her, but was himself in no hurry to eat. As the three of them walked in the direction of the central railway station and turned into a crowded pedestrian street, it was comforting for Tom to see that, unlike Ulrika, Pia did not seem to be in any hurry to rush into the first restaurant she laid eyes on. There were people sitting on the steps of a building that Pia said was where they awarded the Nobel Prizes. In front of the building was a fruit market, but the girls led Tom downstairs to reveal a large indoor market where they were selling fish, tea, herbs, cheeses, and there was even a kebab stand. They moseyed around, building up an appetite, and by the time they resurfaced, they were discussing where to eat. The girls seemed to be keen on Chinese and Tom was happy to surrender to their culinary taste and judgment. The restaurant they chose was a Chinese buffet, where upon payment, you received a plate that you could potentially fill up until closing time. One drink was included but there was a limitless supply of water - potentially. After a few spoonfuls, Ulrika, who had been relatively quiet until then, burst into conversation, asking Tom about his impression of Stockholm, and telling him that she thought there was much more to do in Stockholm than Helsinki.

"You can't really see Stockholm in a day," she said, "but you can see Helsinki in less than a day. In fact, we didn't even see Helsinki when we went there. We stayed in our cabin until it was time to come back. We partied the whole night and slept the whole day."

After several helpings, they left satisfied in the knowledge that they would not need to eat for another week. Pia had paid for Tom's food at her mother's request, for which Tom was grateful. This was from a woman who would have turned him away in the rain had it not have been for a fuse popping out, giving Tom the opportunity to save the day and Pia time to persuade her to let him stay. After several hours of strolling around places that Pia and Ulrika thought represented the beauty of Stockholm, they pointed to a red and white ship dwarfing other vessels and said, "That's the ship that is going to Finland. We will be taking the metro back from here. You can take a bus from here to the harbour, or you can walk. It's not very far."

Tom had already been walking a lot, so he thought a few more minutes wouldn't make much difference. Having parted with Pia and her friend Ulrika, Tom walked towards the harbour and was soon at the ticket office where a friendly blonde girl in a red uniform informed him that his Interrail card only gave him a 50% discount on the price of the ticket. She tried to sell him a whole cabin to himself, but he said that he didn't mind sharing with three other people if that meant saving money. Besides, he thought it would be better than spending his time in solitude. Tom took the escalator up and waited for the gates to open. There was still a long time before departure, and very few people had arrived as early as he had. But as the clock clicked closer to departure time, more and more people turned up with bags of various sizes. It was half an hour before departure when the gates opened, and Tom followed the crowd onto the luxurious ship that looked a bit like a casino with all its fruit machines. Tom showed his ticket and cabin key, and was told to take a lift to the lower deck. He followed the numbers down a narrow corridor until he found his cabin. It was a small room with two bunk beds and a small table between them with four chocolate mint sweets on it. Tom took one and put it in the side pocket of his haversack for later. He then inspected the bathroom, which included a shower, toilet and basin. There was a towel on each bed, and there was also a dressing table and mirror in the cabin, along with a rack and hooks for hanging coats near the door. Tom chose a lower bunk bed and slid his haversack under it, followed by his shoes, before lying on the bed to rest while waiting for his cabinmates. Several footsteps passed the cabin before Tom heard the door unlock and saw a man walk in, immediately introducing himself as Sven and extending his hand for a quick shake. He tossed his holdall onto the floor at the end of the remaining bed, claimed the lower bunk by ruffling the pillow, and after hanging up his jacket returned to his bed for a conversation with Tom. Once establishing their common language as English, he wasted no time in telling Tom that he was involved in a huge project that would see the end to public roads as we know them. He said that his proposal had been approved and that within three years there would be a global network of monorail tracks replacing our roads, insisting that it would be very efficient and environmentally friendly. Tom challenged his idea, trying not to openly question his sanity, but Sven always had an answer. So, he wished him luck and headed up on deck.

The ship had already set sail, and the beauty of the archipelago in the calm sea gave Tom a feeling of tranquillity that drained away his tiredness. The regular travellers had seen it all before and were more interested in the tax-free shop. After a while, Tom began to feel a chill in the air and decided it was time to explore the ship's interior. There was a self-service restaurant with several televisions where people could take their food and follow the news to see what had happened in the hour since they had left Swedish soil. There was also a room with reclining chairs where once again people could watch television or even sleep. For entertainment, there was a disco with everything but people and a nightclub, which was where the passengers were turning to for music and drink. Tom took another walk around the ship to see if he had missed anything, and by the time he returned to the nightclub there were even more people there, creating a much better atmosphere. He scanned the large dimly lit room for a potential dancing partner until his eyes met a vision in red and could go no further. She was standing there with her long blond hair, dressed from top to toe in red, and as their eyes met, she smiled, but she was not alone. A young blond man wearing a striped shirt and tie was in her company. There could be no one else Tom would want to dance with that night, so he walked towards the exit, passing her on his way and sneaking a smile, which she reciprocated. Moments later, with not much else going on, Tom returned to the nightclub only to see that the blond man had gone to the bar to buy a drink, leaving the girl in red alone. Tom went up to her and said, "If you didn't have a boyfriend, I'd ask you to dance with me."

Without a moment's hesitation, the girl replied, "I'm not with that pig. Let's dance." She held Tom's hand and led him to the dance floor, where they danced until the proverbial cows came home, but Tom only learned that her name was Satu. He had asked several other questions, but she was finding it difficult to hear him over the music. When the dancing ended, they went on deck, where Satu's blond hair was glistering as he held her in his arms, but she still had trouble hearing or understanding him. As they exchanged addresses under the moonlight, she told Tom that she was from Tampere, but was studying at Helsinki

University, and would like to get to know him better on land, "Not like two sheep that pass in the night," she said with a smile. She explained that some friends would be giving her a lift to Tampere the next morning, and she would be waiting for Tom to arrive by train in the evening.

As they walked in from the deck, Satu said that she needed to powder her nose, and after a while, Tom decided to pay a quick visit to the gents. When he returned, he waited for a while, but she was taking much longer than expected. Finally, he asked a girl to go in and call her name, but the girl returned to say that the toilets were empty. He went back on deck to where they had been together, but she had vanished. Tom walked around the ship with his eyes peeled until there were not many passengers awake. Finally, he returned to his cabin and the snoring Sven, where the sweet scent of Satu sent him to sleep wondering why she had disappeared.

Day 19 Friday

The next morning, when Tom woke up, the cabin was in total darkness except for the light seeping in from under the door, which had guided Sven to the bathroom for his morning shower without having to switch the cabin light on. Tom got ready and waited for his turn to use the bathroom, greeting Sven as they swapped rooms. When he returned, fresh and ready to go, Sven had long left, so he scooped up the unclaimed chocolate mint sweets, threw his haversack over his shoulder and left the cabin, only closing the door when he had looked back to make sure he had not left anything behind. As he disembarked, he looked around for Satu, but he was among the last passengers to leave the ship, and she wasn't. There was a train taking passengers from the harbour to the city. The train was continuing on to Tampere, but Satu had said that she would be expecting him in the evening, so Tom got off the train after its three-minute journey to spend some hours in the city of Turku. He had taken only a few steps when he heard a voice address him in French. A girl with light brown hair had just got off the same train. Tom informed her that he did not speak French.

"I'm studying French at the university here in Turku," said the girl, "I just wanted to practice a bit." She introduced herself as Tuire and explained that she had just been visiting her friend in Stockholm. She then asked Tom how long he would be staying in Turku. When he said that he would be leaving Turku later that day, she offered to show him around, adding, "As long as I can stop off at my flat for a small breakfast first, you can join me if you haven't eaten." Tuire asked Tom which ship he had been on and whether he had enjoyed his trip. She was glad to hear that he had been on the same ship as her and told him that the other company had a bad reputation for racism and even the occasional violence against passengers.

She said, "Since my friend Sari moved to Sweden, I have become a regular traveller to Stockholm. The first time I travelled there, the waiter on the ship poured beer all over me. He didn't even apologise to me and when I complained, the manager said, "These things happen. Get used to it." At first, I thought it was an accident, but my friends said that it could have been racially motivated, as I was talking to an Algerian man at the time. I will never use that company again. We were on the same ship last night, but I went to bed early because I'd been celebrating in Sweden the night before."

"What were you celebrating?" asked Tom.

"Nothing

and everything," she replied. "When we haven't seen each other for a while, we meet up and celebrate all the good things that have happened to us. We get together with a bunch of people and have fun. We all have to say something good that has happened to us recently. One guy said that his mother had been cured of cancer and a girl was celebrating because she had met a very special guy; another said that he had found a coin in the street. We celebrated for him too. Sari said that she was celebrating because I was visiting her, and I said that I was celebrating because I have such a good friend. It's just a good way to start a party. It almost guarantees that we are still in a happy mood when we get drunk."

At that moment, Tuire turned into a building, and Tom followed. They took the lift up to her flat, which Tom found surprisingly tidy for a student's flat. They walked into a room with a bed, a desk and one chair. The other room, apart from the bathroom, was a small kitchen. Tuire boiled some water and opened a jar of granulated tea, which they enjoyed with tubed fish paste on crispbread before heading off to the city centre. They looked in some shops near the market square, where elderly locals were buying vegetables, and went to see the indoor market where, Tom bought some pastries for later. Tuire said that she had some discount coupons for her favourite pizzeria and suggested they could eat there. The pizza was excellent, and a weak beer was included in the price, making it an even better deal. After their meal, they walked along the river for a while before heading back to Tuire's flat for Tom to pick up his haversack. Tuire said that she was meeting up with a friend and took Tom to the music library near a river, where he listened to music before going to the station. The train left on time and probably for the first time since Paris there were more locals than backpackers on the train.

About two hours later, the train was at Tampere station, and Tom set off to find where Satu lived. He was informed that the address was a 20-minute bus ride from the station. He showed the address to the bus driver and was told where to get off. It was a quiet cul-de-sac with modern houses. Tom rang the doorbell corresponding to the house number on the paper he was holding, but it was only after ringing for the third time that the door opened. A bald man stood there, looking at Tom with disdain. Tom explained that he had come to see Satu, but the man appeared to be having difficulty hearing and understanding him. When Tom showed the man the address in Satu's handwriting and said that she was expecting him, the man replied in broken English that he was her father and that she was in Helsinki for the weekend. Tom asked if he could use their toilet, and the man reluctantly allowed him into the house.

To the left of the bathroom was a room with a single bed covered by a red bedspread with two red cushions, and in the bathroom, there was a red toothbrush and red towels that Tom assumed belonged to Satu. Tom was sure that Satu would be arriving later that evening, but when her father said that he couldn't wait for her there, he asked what the latest time was that he could phone to see if she had arrived. There wasn't much to do in that area, so after walking around a bit, Tom decided to take the bus back to town. It was Friday night and there were several youngsters on the bus dressed up for a night on the town. Among them, two girls caught Tom's eye. He struck a conversation with them, and they asked if he would like to hang out with them. They were Niina, a tall blonde girl who could easily have been a model, and Terhi. Niina was the more stylish of the two, wearing black trousers covering her long legs and a black cardigan revealing a white blouse while Terhi favoured green, which gave her a somewhat military look. They said that they were going to a have a few drinks in town before moving on to a disco, and Tom thought it would be a good way to spend his time before making his phone call to see if Satu had returned home. The pub the girls had chosen was close to the station and had a rather good atmosphere compared to other places, Tom was told. They drank enough to feel good, without jeopardising their chances of getting into a disco. When the time came, Tom walked down to the station to make his phone call. Satu's father said she had called from Helsinki to say that she would not be home that weekend, leaving Tom with the choice of taking the train to Helsinki and arriving at one o'clock in the morning with nowhere to stay, or going to the disco and getting less than two hours sleep on the train, arriving in Helsinki first thing in the morning. The latter seemed more appealing, so he

128

returned to the pub where the girls were ready to leave, and walked with them to the disco feeling a bit awkward, as he had his luggage with him. The bouncer at the door gave Tom, with his haversack, a funny look until he left it at the cloakroom. The girls said he probably thought they were smuggling in cheap alcohol. Upstairs, the disco consisted of a large room for dancing, a circular balcony with chairs and tables overlooking the dance floor and a smaller bar area. Niina, who claimed that she was half Russian and believed that her heritage made her immune to alcohol, was eager to move onto the stronger stuff and returned from the bar with a black drink for Tom to try. They downed their drinks, which tasted like salted liquorice, and boogied onto the dance floor, where after several fast dances, the music changed to slow and Niina fell into the arms of Tom, forcing Terhi to withdraw to the bar. When the slow dances finished, Tom and Niina walked hand in hand to where Terhi was standing, but she was cold and unfriendly talking only to Niina angrily in Finnish. Within minutes, Terhi was on her way out, and Niina said that she too had to leave, as she couldn't let her best friend travel home alone. Tom decided to stay until closing time and soon found himself dancing with a flirtatious Finn called Sirkka who even made fast dances seem slow, wording the lyrics to him suggestively. Closing time was signalled by the music suddenly stopping and all the lights coming on. Tom and Sirkka went down to the cloakroom, where he collected his haversack and told her that he would be catching the next train to Helsinki, but as they walked towards the station, Sirkka mentioned that she lived nearby and that he could sleep at her place. It was a small flat with a bed, an old wobbly table and two chairs in the main room. By that time Tom, who had had a few drinks without eating since lunchtime, had developed a splitting headache.

Neither he nor Sirkka had any painkillers, so he finished off the pastries he had bought from Turku, and Sirkka joined him in a cup of tea before going to bed.

Day 20 Saturday

When Tom woke up in the morning, his headache was gone, and so was Sirkka. He could hear that she was just finishing her shower, so he got ready and waited for his turn to use the bathroom. After some cheese and cucumber sandwiches with tea, Tom walked over to the station and took the train to Helsinki.

Satu's flat was quite a walk from the station, but Tom didn't mind the walk; he wanted to see as much of the Finnish capital as possible. A clapped-out old lift that looked like a cage took him to the third floor of a building close to a cemetery and soon after he rang the doorbell, a little old lady opened the door. When Tom told her that he had come to see Satu, she said that Satu had told her that she was going to Tampere straight from Stockholm and would return to Helsinki on Saturday or Sunday. Tom explained that he had just come from Tampere, where Satu's father had said that she had phoned from Helsinki to say that she would not be going to Tampere that weekend.

"Come in," the old lady said. "You can wait a bit in case she turns up."

It was a spacious flat with several bedrooms as far as Tom could make out. The door to one of the bedrooms was open, showing a bed with a red cover and a desk with a red chair.

The old lady said that she was about to have lunch and would like it if Tom would join her. She spoke good English and said that she was eager to practice. She pulled out a fish casserole from the oven and served it with beetroot salad and placed a jug of elderberry juice on the table. Tom went to the bathroom to wash his hands where he saw a red toothbrush and a red towel. During lunch, the old lady mentioned that Satu would often be given a lift to university by a man driving a red car.

"She is a mysterious girl," the old lady added. "There is something eerie about her. When my husband died two years ago, I decided to take a lodger to keep me company. My daughter is living in Italy and comes to visit whenever she can, so I wanted to keep one room for her and rent the other spare room out to a student. Satu answered the ad I had put in the newspaper, and although I had given her a choice between the two rooms, she ignored the room that was slightly bigger and brighter, and was immediately drawn to the other room, saying that she felt something there. This was the room where my husband had died. We slept in different rooms because of his snoring. One night he suffered a massive heart attack in his sleep and never woke up. Satu was attracted to that room but insisted on bringing her own red curtains. Something about her gives me the shivers."

Tom said he wanted to see a bit more of Helsinki and would phone from the harbour to see if there was any news from Satu before deciding whether or not to go to Tallinn that day. He left Satu a note, thanked the old lady and walked towards the city centre and the harbour. There was a long park between two sides of a street leading to the harbour where people were sitting on benches and picnicking on the grass. Tom watched a magician perform magic and then went through an indoor market to the harbour where he phoned the old lady who told him that Satu had phoned from Tampere, where she would be spending the weekend. There was a ferry leaving for Tallinn shortly, so Tom quickly bought a ticket and minutes later was sitting by the window looking at

Helsinki getting smaller. He was deep in thought, trying to make sense of the Satu mystery when a voice addressed him. It was an American asking if the seat opposite him was taken. He said that his name was Mick and that he had flown in to spend a few days in Helsinki before visiting some of the former Soviet Union countries. He told Tom that he had planned to stay in a very cheap hotel in Tallinn, but had changed his mind because he had a date with a fat Estonian girl called Margaret, and said that he would rather stay at a youth hostel in the old town near where he was meeting the girl and where he would be closer to a pub he had read about in his guidebook. He admitted that he had not met the girl; it was a blind date set up for him by two men he had met at a pub in Helsinki.

"I like fat girls," he said. "Fat girls are fun, cause they don't run."

Tom found this strange but didn't say anything. Just before reaching Tallinn, Tom thought he would try the cheap hotel, so he wrote the address down and said that he would meet up with Mick later. The hotel was a large building at the end of a disused railway track near a dockyard. It was indeed cheap, and when Tom walked up the stairs and into his third-floor room, he could see why. There were four beds with stained pillows and worn-out blankets in a room that seemed to have been neglected by cleaners since the days of communism. Having left his luggage in the room, Tom returned to town to find Mick. He went to the youth hostel, but Mick was not there, so after looking around in the old town with its quaint little shops and cafes and picking up a hamburger, he found the pub that Mick had mentioned and walked in to see Mick sitting on a stool playing the guitar he had brought over with him from the States. Two girls were looking at him adoringly as he sang softly to the tune on his guitar. With

Tom's arrival, Mick finished off his song and put his guitar away in its case. One of the girls hurried out of the pub, leaving the other one with Mick and the newly arrived Tom. Mick ordered beers for himself and Tom, which the landlord said were on the house as a gesture of appreciation for entertaining his customers. Mick and the girl gazed into each other's eyes, drinking their beer without uttering a word until it became too much and they stood up and left the pub together as if in a state of hypnoses. Tom had just finished his beer when a young man walked over with a beer in his hand and said, "I saw your friend walk off with that girl, and thought, if total strangers can be together, what am I waiting for? I have been with my girlfriend for three years, so I proposed to her and she accepted. This beer is for you to celebrate with us, as it was your friend who made this possible." Tom was happy to join in the celebrations and had a smile on his face when he left the pub, but as he got on the tram, he remembered the dreadful hotel he was staying at. The hotel was in a deserted area and as Tom walked in the dark of the night, he held in his pocket the opened up Swiss Army knife that Solveig's father had given him, with the blade ready for self-defence. Tom walked past the unattended reception area of the hotel and straight up to the third floor along the dark corridor that resembled a deserted mental hospital and into his room. The bare 40-Watt bulb hanging in his room was the only source of light and he realised that he had not seen or heard a single guest or member of staff since paying for the room. The only toilet seemed to be on the ground floor. He laid out his sleeping bag on the bed to protect him from the many creatures he was sure had made his bed their home, and took out a dirty t-shirt from his laundry bag to cover the pillow and switched the light out hoping that he would not be visited by rats in the dark. His head had barely touched his t-shirt when he heard a knock on the door. He ignored the knock, but it got louder and more persistent, so he opened the door brandishing the blade of his Swiss Army knife. A woman on the other side fled without a word and Tom got back to bed, hoping there would be no more late-night visits.

Day 21 Sunday

Tom was relieved the next morning to wake up without any bites on his body. He shook his sleeping bag and t-shirt vigorously before packing them and going down for breakfast. There was a small restaurant on the ground floor, but as Tom passed the reception booth, he heard a guest being quoted four times what he himself had paid for one night. It was still cheap, but unfair, so he showed the receptionist his receipt and asked why the new guest was being asked for more. The receptionist looked at Tom's receipt and adjusted the other guest's receipt charging him the correct amount. The new guest was an Englishman called Dave, who thanked Tom by buying him breakfast at the hotel's restaurant. Dave said that he thought the hotel was a cradle of crime when he saw the receptionist in a booth behind what looked like bullet-proof glass, though with such low prices and so few guests there couldn't be much money in the till.

He said, "I knew what to expect because I was told about this hotel by an African man who stayed here for a while when he first came to Tallinn. He told me that one night he got a visit from a prostitute. He was willing to pay for her services, but she and her accomplice robbed him in his room. He continued to stay at the hotel because it was dirt cheap, but he got himself a gun for protection. I just want a cheap hotel; it doesn't matter how dirty or dangerous it may be. I live for danger. It gives me a buzz."

After breakfast, Tom walked to town. He felt much safer in the daylight and was glad to put the grey concrete building of the hotel behind him. The tourist office in the old town was Tom's next port of call, where he inquired about getting to Riga. His Interrail card was not valid in the Baltic countries, so he opted for the coach, which seemed to be a more popular choice among locals. There were several large department stores near the old town where Tom spent the next hours looking around, watching people spend their money buying a variety of items, some of which he was sure they didn't really need. Tallinn seemed like a nice place with interesting people, but Tom didn't want to spend too much time in the Baltic countries where he could not make use of his Interrail card. Not knowing exactly how much time he needed to walk to the coach station, he allowed himself plenty of time, arriving early enough to find the correct bay after purchasing his ticket, becoming one of the first passengers to board coach. He took a window seat behind a girl who had music plugged into her ears and was reading a book, completely cutting herself off from the rest of the world. A grim-looking woman occupied a seat on the other side of the aisle, while three young boys at the back of the coach were making one another laugh with funny remarks in Estonian about passers-by. A woman, quite well dressed but with a visible moustache, got on the coach and spoke briefly with the driver who got off and threw two big suitcases into the luggage hold before slamming it shut. The woman got on the coach and chose a seat close to the three boys, who to Tom's surprise did not react to the latest passenger and sat relatively quietly as the coach pulled out of its bay and drove off towards Riga. Tom, having forsaken lunch in favour of a late meal in Riga, was already feeling hungry, so he delved into his haversack and pulled out the chocolate he had been carrying around with him since Germany. As he lay back in his reclining seat, breaking off and biting into several rows of chocolate, he noticed that the landscape was distinctly different from what he had experienced in the Nordic countries. When the girl in front of him stood up to reach for her holdall in the overhead rack, their eyes met, and he offered her some chocolate to break the ice. She showed more interest in Tom than in the chocolate, turning round in her seat to ask him what he was doing in that part of the world and what he had seen in Tallinn. She mentioned that she was from a village near a seaside town about two hours away from Tallinn.

"I found a job in Tallinn and was sharing a flat with two other girls. I loved it there, until the company I was working for said that I would have to work more hours for less money. I couldn't afford my share of the rent, so I quit my job and moved back to live with my parents. My friends found another girl to share the flat with, but I sometimes go there for weekends or to look for work. If I do find work there, I'll move back in with them. There will be less room, but my share of the rent will be less too."

They were deep in conversation when the coach crossed a bridge into a small town and stopped at a small station. The girl handed Tom a small book and asked him if he would like to exchange addresses, before getting off the coach and walking straight over to a bus stop. A few minutes later, the girl who was still waiting at the bus stop gave Tom a wave as the coach pulled out of the station. Having no one to talk to for the rest of the journey, Tom was relieved when he saw the lights of Riga, indicating that he would soon be reaching his destination. At the station Tom watched as a man, a woman and two children joyfully greeted and hugged the grim-looking woman, who took it all in her stride without changing her facial expression. It was beginning to get late so Tom checked in at a hotel not too far from the station. It was by no means a hotel he would recommend to anyone he might see again. There was a communal toilet and shower in the corridor near his room, which overlooked a noisy street with its bright lights clearly visible through the thin curtains. A squeaky bed with stained bed linen and a cracked sink was in character with the rest of the hotel. As Tom left his room to venture into town, he saw the tall, unmistakeable figure of Mick walk into one of the rooms along the corridor, so he walked up to the door and banged on it, shouting "Police," changing his voice slightly.

When Mick opened the door, Tom said, "The police said I'd find you here."

Mick stood speechless with his eyebrows raised until Tom explained that he was staying in a room at the end of the corridor and asked if he would like to grab a bite to eat. Mick grabbed his jacket and off they went to explore Riga, or at least the areas closest to their hotel. Mick had already spent several hours in Riga and had only gone back to his hotel to fetch his jacket in case it got chilly. They strolled along a pedestrian street not far from the hotel, watching couples walking hand in hand and looking in shop windows.

"What happened with your fat date yesterday?" Tom asked jokingly.

"Don't talk to me about dates," Mick said shaking his head. "I was told that when I get to Tallinn, I should ask for fat Margaret. Everyone I asked pointed towards a tower just outside the old town. When I got closer, I started scanning the crowd for a fat girl, but then found out that Fat Margaret was actually the name of the tower itself. I was very disappointed, but the girl in the pub almost made up for it. When we left the pub, we took a cab back to her apartment and did a lot of kissing until she told me it was the wrong time of the month for her to go any further. I was almost in tears when I left her apartment."

A pub that served food caught their eye, and they sauntered in to check the menu. The pub had a yard where they sat and ordered food and drink.

While they were waiting, Mick said, "Last time I was in England, I had just arrived and really felt like having a beer, so I went to a pub and was sitting at a table outside enjoying my second beer when I heard a short shriek behind me and saw a man with a baseball bat in his hand covered in blood fall to the ground. Above him was a man holding a bloody knife in his hand. The man pulled me by the arm and said, "Let's go! Your life is in danger." I grabbed my baggage and ran from the scene, which was directly opposite a police station. We went to his apartment where I stayed for my entire vacation. He told me he had seen a man sneak up behind me with a baseball bat and was just about to hit me over the head when he stabbed him. The man who was Irish, said that I could stay with him as long as I kept buying him Guinness. We drank quite a bit during my stay with him. I never found out why that man wanted to attack me, but it seems wherever I go, bad luck follows me."

Tom said that he would be going to Vilnius the next day, but Mick said that he had read about a seaside town in Lithuania called Palanga, and persuaded Tom to go with him. He said that they could cut costs by sharing a room. After eating, they walked around Riga a bit before going back to the hotel to get some sleep.

Day 22 Monday

Early the next morning, having finally managed to sleep through what sounded like a party behind his door, Tom woke up and quickly got ready to leave. Mick was coming out of the bathroom as Tom walked into the corridor, and minutes later they left the hotel. There was a corner shop next to the hotel where they bought breakfast before walking down to the coach station. On the way to the station, Mick broke wind several times, proudly announcing each time, "That was a good one." Tom thought it might not be a good idea to share a room with this anal trumpeter but hoped it was just something in the Riga air that had made him act so childishly. On the coach, they began to eat what they had just bought, trying to make as little mess as possible. They had occupied the row of seats at the back of the coach. At 190 cm tall, Mick had been worried that there might not be enough legroom for him on the coach, but there was plenty of space at the back both for his legs and his guitar, which he treasured more than the rest of his luggage put together. He said that if he ever ran out of money, he could take out his guitar and busk until he had enough money for a meal.

"It doesn't take long," he said. "Once back home, I was in a park, sitting on a bench enjoying the beautiful weather we were having, when I just felt like playing on my guitar. As I was playing and singing to myself, a wealthy woman came up to me and asked if I had ever sung to an audience. Of course, I had played to small audiences, but I thought she meant at a venue, so I instinctively said "No." She said, "Come with me then." She looked out of place in the park with her jewelry and stylish designer clothes, but we were soon in her chauffeur-driven car. I had never felt so comfortable in a car, with its exquisite leather seats and ample legroom.

"We were driven through gates into a long driveway leading to a house that looked more like a mansion. Well, I suppose it was a mansion. She took me in and said, "Poor thing. You must be starving. After you've eaten, you can have a shower and get out of these rags. I'll get you a manicure to make you look half human." She took me to the kitchen and told her manservant to feed me. He was a short man with a big moustache and was dressed like a chef without the hat. He took out a big steak, which he prepared for me with fries, vegetables and a lovely sauce he made on the spot. He opened a bottle of red wine for me too. After I had eaten, the woman came to the kitchen and said, "When you've had enough, go wash your face and meet me upstairs in my bedroom with your instrument." I thought it was strange but did as she had instructed. There were several rooms upstairs, but her bedroom was the one with the open door. She was sitting on a king-size bed and smiled when I walked in. "Are you ready to do what I brought you here for? Come join me here on the bed and do what you do best, but take it out slowly. You don't want to frighten him," she said, pointing to a dozy little dog in a basket. "Fluffy Johnston hasn't been feeling himself lately. Your kind of music is just the thing to cheer him up." I asked her if the dog had any favourite songs, but she looked at me as if I were stupid, so I started to play The Beatles. You can't go wrong with The Beatles. But the dog didn't react. I tried other artists, but nothing happened. After about ten minutes of singing various songs, the woman got up and shouted, "Stop! You're garbage. You can't even stimulate a dog." She then called her driver and said, "Take the tramp back to his bench in the park."

"The car didn't feel so comfortable on the way back. I kept on thinking how things could have been different if I had sung "How much is that doggie in the window" and Elvis Presley's "Hound Dog". It was ludicrous that she mistook me for a tramp. I was clean and well-dressed enough, to go on a date. In fact, I was on a date. I had arrived an hour early to make the most of the good weather, but by the time the driver dropped me off, my date had come and gone. We had been dating for almost a year, so I thought she would understand when I told her what had happened, but she said, "You don't have to make up stories if you don't want to be with me." She had wanted us to get married, but I told her that I didn't want to rush into things. After that episode, she said that we should take a break. I should travel the world and sew my wild oats, then see how we feel about each other in a year's time. I'm going to see as much as Europe as I can and then head down to Africa and maybe catch a bit of Asia too."

Almost as soon as Tom and Mick got off the coach at Palanga coach station, they were approached by a woman in her late 60s early 70s who said that her name was Maria and asked them if they were looking for somewhere to stay. The price was reasonable so they went to see the room, which was part of a house with a garden and an outside toilet in the backyard - if you can call a hole in the ground a toilet. It was a large room with beds in opposite corners and a window facing the garden. They took the room and paid for one night upfront. Mick changed into something more comfortable and went down to the garden with his guitar to relax by sitting on a chair under a tree and singing some of his favourite songs. Some of the other guests including two children were already in the garden and Tom watched from the window as Maria complimented the talented Mick in broken English. Tom went down to the garden and told Mick that he thought they should go to the beach. Mick took his guitar back to the room while Tom waited for him in the garden. It was a short walk to the sandy beach, which seemed to be a popular resort. Tom and Mick walked along the beach eyeing the girls and making mental notes of which ones they would like to approach. A group of boys were starting a game of beach football and looking for more players, so Tom volunteered himself and Mick, but Mick, who ended up in Tom's team, was not a fan of football - or soccer as he called it - and walked off after a few minutes. Tom was a keen footballer and didn't mind taking on the burden of being a man short and even ended up the unofficial man of the match, scoring four goals including the winner at the end. After the match, Tom noticed that a girl he had seen earlier had been watching at least the last minutes of the match. They spoke for a while and agreed to meet later that evening. She had light hair and a slightly pointy nose with a few freckles and said that her name was Vaida and came from a small town not very far from there. On the way back Tom saw that Mick was playing beach volleyball and signalled to him that he was going back to the room. As soon as he walked through the gates Maria noticed him and called him over. She explained in broken English that a family who were regular customers of hers were arriving for a week that evening and wanted to stay in their usual room, which was the one Tom and Mick had occupied. She apologised and said that she would refund their money. Tom said that they were leaving very early the next morning and that it was too late for them to find alternative accommodation, so she said that they could stay in her living room that night. Maria's living quarters had a separate entrance at the back of the building, opening to the kitchen with the living room to the left. There were two settees, which would serve adequately for the night, so Tom collected his things from his room and moved them to Maria's living room where she refunded his share of the payment for the room. Tom went back into the garden and saw Mick arriving from the beach.

He went up to him and said, "I've been talking with Maria; she told me that she wants you in her room tonight for a night of passion. She said that if you were any good, she would pay for it."

Mick looked at Tom dismissively and was about to walk away when Tom caught Maria's eye and asked, "You want him in your room?"

Maria walked towards Mick and said in her broken English, "Yes, tonight my room."

Mick looked horrified with his dropped jaw and boggling eyes, but Tom was not finished and quickly said, "She'll pay for it," turning immediately to Maria and saying, "Money?" while making the internationally recognised money sign by rubbing his thumb and bent index finger together and pointing his gaze towards Mick.

Maria nodded at Mick and said, "Yes, I give money in room," and walked towards her living quarters to wait for Mick. Tom and the trembling bewildered Mick went to their room where Tom explained everything, to Mick's relief. Mick packed his things and took them to Maria's living room where she was waiting to give him a refund. Mick had read in his guidebook that there was a street in Palanga with several restaurants, one of which had live music, and as they could already hear music, they thought it couldn't be far. Mick got the only spare key and off they went following their ears. The street was indeed easy to find, but almost every restaurant in the bustling street had live music. They chose one of the many restaurants and sat down for their main meal of the day. Tom said that he had a date, so they decided to go their separate ways and meet outside the restaurant at midnight as they only had one key between them and had to get up very early in the morning to catch the coach to Vilnius.

Tom met Vaida at their prearranged meeting place and walked slowly down the street and to the pier. She was wearing a pretty summer dress that brought out the best in her. They walked to the end of the pier and back to the street where they bumped into Mick who was walking hand in hand with a short girl with short black hair, slightly rosy cheeks and round glasses. They acknowledged each other as they passed by.

Mick turned round and said secretly with excitement, "She's a nurse."

Tom said, "See you at midnight."

Vaida had said that the girl she was travelling with had not been feeling well and was in her room, so after exchanging addresses she kissed Tom goodnight and went back to her room, as she said that it would be unfair to leave her friend alone for too long. Tom and Vaida had enjoyed each other's company so much that they had not noticed the passage of time and it was already ten minutes past midnight. Tom rushed to the restaurant where he was to meet Mick, but Mick was not there. The more Tom waited the more he thought that perhaps Mick had gone back to Maria's living room, so he decided to abandon the restaurant and go back to Maria's place as he knew that Mick would eventually end up there. All the lights were off and the door was locked. With the curtains drawn, the only possible view into the living room was from a small side-window, which Tom had to climb to reach, but the room was dark, and he could not make out whether Mick was there or not. He knocked on the window a few times before making a dash to the restaurant and back. The streets were by now empty and remembering Mick's bad-luck stories, Tom began to worry that perhaps a misfortune had befallen him. He seriously considered going to the police, but the nearest police station was half an hour away by car, according to some passers-by. It was just before three o'clock when Mick appeared, looking rather surprised to see Tom sitting on the doorstep in the dark. He said that he had decided to stay out late, thinking that Tom would surely somehow find his way into the living room. There were only a few hours left before they had to be on their way to Vilnius.

Day 23 Tuesday

Early the next morning, Tom and Mick woke up to catch the first coach to Vilnius. "Jesus, she was a nurse," said Mick, rubbing his eyes, as if it had all been a dream. They quickly packed their things and quietly left Maria's house, leaving her spare key on the kitchen table. They had just reached the coach station when Mick, who had been quiet the whole time, turned to Tom and said, "She was no oil painting, but she was a nurse. Nurses know all about the human body. And that includes men's pleasure points. This is an opportunity of a lifetime! I'm going to stay here another day and look for the nurse."

Tom got on the coach and looked out of the window to see the tall figure of Mick standing there with his big nose and short-cropped hair. He could see something in his brown eyes that he hadn't seen before. It was a mixture of hope, love and despair all rolled up into one big softie. Tom chose to sit at the back of the coach, hoping to catch up on lost sleep from the previous night, but he wasn't alone for long.

A tall sporty-looking girl with long fair hair, carrying a holdall in one hand and a bunch of rolled-up drawings under the other arm, walked up to the end of the coach and carefully placed her drawings in the overhead rack and positioned her holdall strategically to protect them from any other luggage, though most of the other passengers were seated at the front or middle of the coach. As she sat down, Tom acknowledged her presence with a smile and asked, "Are you an artist?"

"Well, I wouldn't call myself an artist; I just love art," she said with a smile. She had a warm friendly voice and a sparkle in her eyes that enhanced her beauty. She said that her name was Kristina.

"I love coming to Palanga, because there are so many foreign and Lithuanian tourists with interesting faces to draw. Every face has a story that I try to capture. When you take a picture of someone, you capture their reflection as it is, but when you draw or paint someone's portrait you can bring out their inner feelings such as anxiety, love, hope or loneliness. I don't think I've mastered that yet. That's why I don't call myself an artist."

Tom asked to see her work and was very impressed with what he saw.

"It's a good way to earn money," he said.

"I do it for the love of it, but I make money too. Sometimes people ask me to draw or paint their portraits and pay me for it, but I prefer to draw people without asking them. It's more natural that way, and often they are happy to pay for it, but it doesn't matter if they don't. I make enough money to live a simple life for now, but I made a lot last year. I was sitting outside a restaurant, drinking a cup of tea and watching people go by when a man got out of a car, walked over, snapped his fingers at the waitress and said, "Spaghetti". I had never seen such arrogance. When the food arrived, he said, "Beer," with a dismissive frown. He was so arrogant that he could hardly be bothered to talk. As he sat there forking his food with disinterest, as if he was doing the world a favour by eating to keep himself alive, I could see his shiny car parked in the background. I thought it would make a great picture, so I began to draw. I made sure he didn't notice me drawing him, as he did not look like the kind of person who would take kindly to anyone invading his space or even looking at him. I had just finished drawing when he suddenly got up, threw some money on the table, and left.

He got into his car and drove off as if he owned the road. About two months later, some jewellery shops had been robbed. The police had a description of the gang members and the number plate of the getaway car. They were hopeful of finding the thieves through the number plate, but then they found the car abandoned somewhere and realised that it had been stolen. When I saw the picture of the men on television, I recognised the gang leader as the man I had drawn at the restaurant. I had also drawn his car with its number plate, so I informed the police, and they caught him. The insurance company gave me a reward that was by far the most I had ever earned from any painting I had done before."

Kristina seemed puzzled when Tom mentioned that he would be taking the train from Vilnius to Warsaw that day.

"Why don't you get off in Kaunas where I get off and take the train from there? It's probably the same one."

Tom looked at his book of timetables and saw that her suggestion made sense. When they arrived in Kaunas, Tom had a few hours to kill before his train was due to leave. Kristina offered to show him her town if they could first drop her paintings off at her flat. Tom helped carry some of her paintings, and when they reached her flat, she asked him in for a cold drink. There were some paintings on the wall and an easel in the middle of the floor, with a cloth draped over it concealing an unfinished painting. She said that she didn't want anyone to see her paintings before they were ready.

"Not even me," she said. "I have the finished picture in my mind and that's what I want to see."

After their cold drink, they walked into the old town. Kristina said she would like to take Tom to a place where two rivers meet. She said that it was a place where she often sat down to paint, but this time, they sat down for some Lithuanian meatloaves. On the way to the train station, they went shopping together. Kristina needed food since she had been away, and Tom wanted something to keep him going on the train. Tom had taken some pictures of his time in Kaunas, but Kristina said that she had all the pictures in her head and would paint a picture of Tom for him to see next time they met. As Tom boarded the train, he said he looked forward to seeing her again soon.

The train was crowded with international travellers, and once again he could hear several people speaking English in various accents, which was quite comforting after the coach trips he had taken, where most of the other passengers were locals who didn't look as if they could understand any English.

Tom was sinking into his seat with tiredness from lack of sleep when he heard a voice say, "Can you help a little Polish girl with her bag?" He looked up and saw a girl with light brown shoulder-length hair stretching to reach a holdall on the rack above his head. She took a few things out of the bag and then asked him to put it back. Among the things she had kept were some well-wrapped sandwiches.

"Would you like a sandwich?" she asked. "They're homemade Lithuanian sandwiches."

Tom took a sandwich and asked her if she was going all the way to Warsaw. She said her name was Ania and that Warsaw was her hometown.

"I was skiing near the Czech border last winter, when I twisted my ankle and had to spend the rest of my vacation resting. That's when I met a kind gentle Lithuanian man who kept me company while I was recovering. We talked about philosophy, which is what I am studying at university, and enjoyed good food and wine. When I got back to Warsaw and he to Vilnius, we corresponded for a while and decided we would like to see each other, so he invited me to Vilnius. I was very excited and looking forward to seeing him. He met me at Vilnius station with a strong smell of alcohol on his breath. This didn't bother me much at first, but as soon as we were in his flat, he poured himself and me a drink. I told him it was a bit too early for me to drink, so he downed them both and then poured himself another. The more he drank, the more unpleasant he became, until it reached a point where I really didn't feel safe with him. I had no choice but to leave.

"There were no trains back to Warsaw until the following morning. I was sitting at the station crying, when a woman sat next to me and asked if I was okay. I told her what had happened, and she said that I could sleep at her place. She was probably in her 50s or maybe early 60s and had a calming effect on me, so I decided to go with her. She lived alone with a black and white cat and had lots of plants in every room, including the bathroom. She made me a cup of herbal tea and assured me that I had done the right thing to leave that drunken man. "I was married to a man for 12 years," she said, "and we had two children together. It was a good marriage, until I started going to yoga classes. He had a well-paid job, so I didn't need to work, but he wanted me to stay at home when he was at work. He said that he wanted me to be at home the whole time, in case our son or daughter came home from school feeling unwell. From then on, our relationship went downhill and ended up in the divorce courts. My yoga and meditation got me through the divorce and helped me recover from it, though without them I would probably still be married. Shortly after our divorce, he met and married a Canadian basketball player. They live in Canada now, with my children, who lived with me to start with but moved there to further their education. I regret not trying to work things out with my husband, but in your case, walking away was definitely the right thing to do."

"The next morning, when I was leaving," Ania continued, "she gave me a bag full of sandwiches she had made while I was getting ready. You are welcome to help yourself to more if you want. I'm only a small Polish girl. I can't eat them all."

They finished off the sandwiches, and Tom had some of the snacks he had bought from Kaunas during the long train journey to Warsaw, where he was planning to visit Agnes. He was even more excited about seeing Margaret in Krakow a day later. When they reached Warsaw, Ania said that she was familiar with the address he was looking for, as a friend of hers was living in the same block of flats which was in walking distance from the railway station, and offered to show him the way. Ania left Tom at the entrance of the building and wished him a pleasant stay in Warsaw.

Tom took the lift up and rang the doorbell, but there was no reply, and he could see that there was no one at home. He hadn't told Agnes exactly when he would be visiting her, so she had probably gone away he thought. It was rather late, and with no other place to stay, the railway station was his only option. But when he got out of the lift, he saw Ania talking to another girl. The girl was her friend from that block of flats, and she confirmed that Agnes and her family had been gone for a few days. Ania said that Tom could stay with her if her parents approved. When they arrived at her flat, Ania's parents were surprised to see her back so soon. She spoke with her parents in Polish for a minute or two before calling Tom over to introduce him to them. Her father was a very short man with a thin moustache, possibly to distinguish him from children, while her mother was a large woman, though below average in height. They both looked very kind and seemed genuinely happy to welcome Tom.

Ania's father had a smattering of English, often pausing for a considerable length of time searching for the right word, which he would then deliver with pride. Her mother disappeared into the kitchen and later appeared with two large bowls of soup. Just as Tom had finished his soup and was about to thank his hosts for a deliciously filling meal, the main course arrived. Ania's mother had been labouring in the kitchen frantically ever since Tom's unannounced arrival. The meal was followed by fruit kompot and apologies for not serving anything special, which Ania translated. Her mother didn't speak any English at all and communicated with smiles, while her father, who had armed himself with a large dictionary, was happy to talk until precisely 11 o'clock, when the little man looked at his watch, slid off his chair and announced that he had to get up early for work the next morning but would see Tom for lunch. When Tom informed him that he would be leaving before lunch, he stepped back in horror, looking at Tom hoping that he would admit it was a joke. But as that did not happen, his horror turned to sadness, and after Tom had shaken his hand to thank him for his hospitality, he quickly retired to his bedroom to avoid showing any deeper emotions. Ania's mother was also saddened by the news that Tom would be leaving the next day and suddenly there was an air of gloom in the room, making Tom feel slightly guilty, but not guilty enough to keep him awake, as he had been struggling on many occasions that day to stay awake after his short sleep the previous night. The huge soft pillow was just the thing to send him straight to dreamland.

Day 24 Wednesday

Tom woke up to the sound of someone turning a key in the front door. It was Ania's mother, who had been shopping. When he got ready and walked into the living room there was an array of Polish sausages and other meaty comestibles laid out on the table in his honour. Ania was not much of an eater, and her mother had already eaten, so it was mainly for Tom, who spent a good hour sampling Polish hospitality while talking to Ania. After breakfast, Ania said that she would take Tom for a bit of sightseeing before taking him to the station. Ania's mother gave Tom a bag full of snacks for the journey and said that he would always be welcome back. Although there wasn't much time for sightseeing, Tom was shown the main sights before walking through a park with Ania to the central station where he thanked her for everything and got on the train to Krakow. Soon after the train had left the station, the conductor came to check the tickets but spent several minutes in discussion with a woman who was trying to convince him of the validity of her ticket.

"This wouldn't happen if there was no money in the world," said the rugged-looking man seated next to Tom.

"How would that work?" asked Tom.

The man continued in his South African accent to explain: "Everything would be free. We would all study or work as we do, but instead of receiving limited payment, we would be able to take what we needed from shops and get on buses and trains or aeroplanes for free. Everyone would have to do something, just like countries where there is no social welfare. There would be hardly any crime. You wouldn't worry about people stealing things from you, and there would only be high-quality goods because unlike now, where manufacturers make poor-quality stuff for people who can't afford the best, in a world without money everyone would make their choices based on quality. A few years ago on my travels, I met an Englishman called Mark who shared his ideology with me. I think it would be great if it one day came true."

"What would stop us taking more than we need, causing a shortage?" asked Tom.

"Having more than you need now could be a sign of success, but in a moneyless world it would be a sign of greed," the rugged-looking man replied with conviction. The discussion continued until Tom went quiet to digest the idea and seemed satisfied with what he had heard.

Just before Krakow, he had some of the snacks Ania's mother had given him, as it was well past lunchtime and he didn't know how long it would take him to find Margaret's flat.

At the station, Tom was told that he should take tram number 25, and on the tram a girl told him when it was time to get off. It was a tall building he couldn't miss. On the sixth floor, a woman with thick glasses opened the door and asked Tom in while calling Margaret, who greeted him with a hug and took him to the living room, where her father was fiddling with something resembling a small engine on some old newspapers strewn over the living room table. He was a thin man with a goatee and shook hands without uttering a word. Margaret said that he was a very quiet man who didn't speak any English, but being an engineer knew a lot of technical words in English. She also said that they were about to visit her grandmother up in the mountains.

"If you had arrived 20 minutes later, I wouldn't have been here. My father is driving me to Zakopane to stay with my grandmother at our summer place. Would you like to come with me?"

Tom accepted the invitation and mentioned that his next port of call would be Bratislava.

"When you want to leave Zakopane we can drive you across the border where you can take the train to Bratislava. You'll like my grandmother. She's a very wise woman," Margaret added.

Within half an hour Tom was sitting in the front seat of a small banger that looked as if it might not make it past the first set of traffic lights, driven by Margaret's father with Margaret herself in the backseat. Margaret and her father had quite a long conversation in Polish forcing Tom into an uncomfortable silence until Margaret switched languages leaving her father to concentrate on his driving. Margaret said that they were discussing a book they had read and began to explain in more detail what they had been discussing, but Polish literature was not one of Tom's strongest subjects, so he was happy when Margaret's father suddenly shouted what sounded like a Polish swearword at a careless driver, prompting Margaret to comment on Polish drivers and their driving habits. Margaret's father quickly calmed down, said something in Polish with a smile, and was quiet for the rest of the journey except for uttering technical words in English from time to time like a man suffering from technical Tourette's syndrome in an attempt to bond with Tom.

When they arrived at the wooden cottage, Margaret's father took in the bags of shopping that had been on the backseat next to Margaret and left almost immediately. Margaret introduced Tom to her grandmother who spoke no English at all - not even technical. She was a serene woman with grey hair and a friendly demeanour that made Tom feel welcome. Margaret began to put some of the shopping away and prepare food while her grandmother set the table. After eating, Margaret said that she would like to go for a walk with Tom and then went to her room to get changed. Tom could hear some noises, which he was sure he had previously heard in Margaret's flat in Krakow, though there had been no cats in the car. She returned from her room wearing a green shirt and a long floral skirt instead of the pink trousers and stripy sweater she had been wearing.

She took Tom out to the garden and led him down the garden path until they reached a stream where she said, "This is my favourite place in the world. That is why I brought you here. Since we said goodbye at the station in Stockholm, I have been thinking a lot about what happened. It has changed my life. I can now tell you that a year ago I met a man who was tall like a pony and had read many books. He swept me off my feet instantly and we soon announced our engagement. We were to get married at the end of this summer, but when I met you, everything changed. I began to fall in love with you and when I kissed you at the station, I knew I could never be with him again. I can't be with any other man, but I can't be with you either. I am a free spirit."

It was then that Tom heard a cat meowing and realised that it had been Margaret the whole time. The cat was out of the bag, so to speak, and Tom was feeling uncomfortable with the situation but somewhat relieved that Margaret had let him off the hook. By the time they were back at the cottage, it was getting dark. Margaret took Tom to a bedroom and said, "This is my bedroom, this is my bed. You can sleep here, and I will sleep in my parents' room. I'm a weak girl and will find it impossible to resist you if we sleep in the same room. I could easily allow you to have your wicked way with me until dawn." Soon after

158

Margaret had left the room, Tom heard what sounded like cats fighting and knew straight away who it was. On his way back from brushing his teeth, Tom saw Margaret's grandmother who smiled and said something to him in Polish. He smiled back and repeated what she had said, hoping it meant goodnight.

Day 25 Thursday

Tom had to get up quite early as Margaret had informed him that a neighbour of hers had volunteered to drive him to the nearest railway station. Margaret and her grandmother had already half finished their breakfast when Tom walked into the main room. He was all ready to leave and did so after nervously eating his breakfast and saying goodbye to Margaret's grandmother who seemed sad to see him go. Margaret took Tom to a nearby cottage where a young man was closing the boot of his car while taking a last deep puff on his cigarette before extinguishing it under the sole of his shoe.

"This is Tobiasz," Margaret said, "he will take you to the railway station."

Tobiasz shook hands with Tom and pulled the seat forward for him to put his luggage on the backseat. As Tobiasz started the car engine Tom thought he heard cat noises in the background but when he looked, he saw Margaret standing there smiling with her head tilted to one side waving him off with only the slightest movement of her curved fingers.

"Margaret is a fine woman," said Tobiasz as he drove away. "She said that you are travelling around Europe by train and would like to go to the railway station. The nearest railway station to us in Poland is in Krakow, but I will smuggle you across the border to Slovakia where they have a railway station that is much closer. Don't worry, I have done this many times before and I have never got caught."

Not getting the reaction he had hoped for, Tobiasz abandoned his warped sense of humour and said, "We should be at Liptovsky Mikulas station just in time for the train to Bratislava, but it's a nice town if you miss the train."

When they arrived, there was only time for Tom to thank Tobiasz for the lift and jump onto the train. It did seem like a nice town, but he had not planned to stay there and knew he would fall behind in his schedule if he gave in to temptation. He walked down a couple of carriages and took a seat opposite a girl who was reading what looked like a local newspaper. She was wearing a navy-blue cotton dress and after leafing through the paper for a few minutes she folded and tossed it on the seat next to her.

Tom smiled and said, "Nothing interesting?"

"No, just the usual stuff," replied the girl. "Someone had left it on the train, so I took a quick look to see if there was anything interesting. It's good to know what's happening in the world. I'm going for a job interview, which I wouldn't be going to if I hadn't been looking in newspapers and magazines."

"Looking in the classified ads for a job isn't the same as keeping up to date with what is happening in the world," commented Tom.

"No, I didn't look in the classified ads. It all began six weeks ago when a friend of mine was visiting me from Bratislava. I was showing her the sights, and we were taking pictures and just having a great time. I remember seeing a middle-aged man with a young girl, walking arm in arm. He was bald with a round figure, and she was slim with long brown hair and was wearing a miniskirt. We saw them several times that day and I commented to my friend that maybe opposites do attract. A few weeks later, I was looking through a magazine when I saw a picture of a man I was sure I had seen before. At first, I couldn't remember where I had seen him, but then I remembered that he was

161

the man with the young girlfriend. The article said that he was the new bank manager at one of the major banks in Bratislava. It was a long article all about him, and there was a picture of his wife too. She was definitely not the young girl I had seen him with that day. I felt as if I had witnessed a crime. I was angry and didn't want to let him get away with it, but I didn't want to break up their marriage, so I wrote to him telling him what I had seen, hoping that he would feel guilty and end his extramarital affair. A few days later he contacted me and begged me not to tell his wife. He said that they had been going through a rough time when he had a fling with a young girl. He said that he had already ended the relationship and patched things up with his wife just in time to celebrate their 25th wedding anniversary. He told me that he appreciated my silence and offered me a job at his bank but said that I would have to apply for the job and have an interview, though he was the one who would make the final decision and would ensure I got the job. I will get paid much more than I was earning as a waitress, and I will have a good future there. My mother said that she didn't like the idea of my getting a job by blackmailing someone, but I didn't actually blackmail him, and I am qualified to do the job. I am confident that I will be an asset to the bank and so I don't feel guilty about it; I just feel lucky to have noticed what I did. I think it was meant to be."

By the time they reached Bratislava, Tom and Veronika had exchanged addresses and said that they would be in touch.

At the station, Tom was approached by a very camp tourist guide who spoke like an American with a hot potato in his mouth asking if he was looking for accommodation and seemed hurt when Tom told him that he was going to Budapest. Tom had just under two hours to wait for his train to Budapest and after eating the sandwiches Margaret's grandmother had made him, with plenty of time still to wait, he decided to see a bit of the city.

It was a hot day and he soon found himself walking into a bar for a cold drink. Two Englishmen were sitting there drinking beer in an otherwise empty bar. One of the men raised his glass slightly when Tom walked in and said, "The beer is great here and you won't believe how cheap it is." Tom checked the price on the menu and saw that it was well within his budget, so he ordered one and was surprised at how tasty and refreshing it was. While Tom was drinking his beer, a local man walked into the bar and ordered a coffee; the Englishman who had recommended the beer suddenly burst into laughter and almost fell off his stool.

"Did you see what that man did? He ordered a cup of coffee. He must be barking mad to order coffee when the beer is so cheap. If I hear an ambulance, I'll know they have come to take him away to a mental hospital."

Luckily the local man didn't seem to understand English and probably thought he was just a rowdy tourist enjoying a pint of beer, even though the Englishman was looking straight at him in disbelief and laughing his head off. At least the local decided to ignore what was going on and concentrate on his coffee. Tom timed his walk back to the station perfectly, arriving five minutes before departure time. It was a warm afternoon and the crowded train made it feel even warmer until the train got underway and the breeze from the open windows made it not only bearable but even quite pleasant. A young man was sitting opposite Tom smiling from ear to ear.

"Is it your first time here?" he asked.

"Yes," said Tom, "but I only stayed long enough for a beer. What about you?"

"It's my second time here. My name's Daniel," he said, shaking Tom's hand firmly." I'm from Madison, Wisconsin, but my parents are originally from Hungary, so I chose Hungary for my studies where I could learn to speak Hungarian properly and look up my roots as well. I met relatives I never knew I had and soon began to feel at home in Hungary; but it was my first time in Europe and I wanted to see a bit more than just Hungary. That is why I came to Bratislava last fall for the first time. I checked into a youth hostel not far from the railway station but didn't spend much time there at all. On the first day, I met a local girl called Ivana, who showed me the sights and later that evening picked me up from the hostel after I had rested a bit, had a shower and a change of clothing. I took her out for a meal, and she took me dancing. The next day she invited me to her place for a homemade meal. We were inseparable during my short stay in Bratislava and we had a magical time together. When I got back to Budapest, I noticed to my horror that I had lost the paper with her contact details. I hadn't given her my address because I knew that I would be moving to a more permanent address soon and promised to contact her when I did. Foolishly I hadn't given her any ways of contacting me, though at the time it felt like the logical way to do it. I couldn't remember her address, no matter how hard I tried; however, I knew how to get to her apartment, so I thought I'd turn up for Christmas and surprise her. But I got a surprise of my own when my mother arrived unexpectedly and said that she had come to spend Christmas with me as it was my first Christmas away from home and she was missing me. When she went back, I got so busy with my studies that I put the thought of visiting Ivana on hold. By the end of the semester, I wasn't even sure that she still wanted to see me, but one night I woke up in a cold sweat

164

with a terrible feeling that something was wrong. I felt that I would lose Ivana if I didn't get to her straight away. I couldn't get back to sleep, so I threw some things into a bag, went to the station and took the early morning train to Bratislava. I went straight to her apartment and knocked on her door to declare my love and claim her for myself before it was too late. I knocked harder and louder, but there was no answer, so I waited for a while before leaving the building and walking the streets around that area hoping to bump into Ivana, or more likely give her time to return to her apartment. I tried again around lunchtime before going for a pizza and ice-cream. It was starting to get cloudy and I thought it might rain, so I went back to the building and sat on the stairs outside her door waiting for her to return. Several people passed me giving me funny looks. It suddenly occurred to me that she might be away on vacation, so when I saw a young girl about to enter the opposite apartment, I asked her if she knew Ivana. She told me that she had only recently moved in and didn't yet know her neighbours. At that moment a smartly dressed man wearing a brown leather jacket walked past us keys in hand and opened the door to Ivana's apartment. In one horrible moment, I imagined Ivana with him and almost blacked out. The neighbour called out and said something to him in her own language. At that moment I probably wouldn't have understood anything even if it had been in English, but I did hear the name Ivana. After a very brief dialogue, he went into the apartment and closed the door. The girl said that he was living there with his girlfriend, but her name was not Ivana. They had been living there for several months and did not know who lived there before them. I wanted to know who the landlord was so that I could ask if she had left a forwarding address, so the girl knocked on his door and after an even shorter dialogue than the first one she told me that they had gotten the apartment through an agency. She wrote the name and address of the agency down on a piece of paper but said that they were already closed for the day. I went to the youth hostel and checked in, so that I could go to the agency the next day. There were many more people at the hostel than during my first visit. In fact, I was probably lucky to get a bed. I was talking with some of the other tourists when a member of staff came looking for me and said that a young lady was waiting for me at reception. I didn't know who it could be as I had not told anyone where I was. When I went to the reception desk, I saw a girl standing there looking rather apprehensive. Something about her looked familiar, though I was sure I had never seen her before. She asked me if I was Daniel and if I knew Ivana.

"When I confirmed my identity, she said, "Thank God I found you. I was looking for you in Budapest and finally found some people at the university who knew you and gave me your address. Your roommate said that you were in Bratislava. I'm Branka, Ivana's sister. She's in hospital where she gave birth to your son in the early hours of this morning. She doesn't know that I went looking for you. "

"I was in shock, but she could tell that I was happy about the news and told me to quickly gather my things. The drive to the hospital seemed to take forever, though in reality it probably took 10-15 minutes. The rain beating down on the windshield helped numb my brain and soothe my nerves. I willed the car forward and crossed my fingers that the traffic lights would stay green. When we reached the hospital, we rushed to the ward and Branka let me go in alone. I saw Ivana sitting up in bed holding my son. She looked as lovely as ever and thrilled to see me. She introduced me to my son whom she was calling Michael.

166

She then gave me a quizzical look and asked me how I had found out about her, at which point Branka stepped forward with a smile. As the two sisters shared a moment together, it all felt so surreal. I knew that Ivana wanted to know why I hadn't been in touch, so I told her the whole story. She said that she had left her apartment and moved back with her parents for the last months of her pregnancy so that she could be with them when the baby was born. I felt bad about not being around during her pregnancy, but I was really glad that I had found her again. That night Branka took me to her parents' house in the countryside. They didn't know that she had found me, so I stayed in the car while she went in to tell them. I was very nervous about meeting the parents for the first time. I didn't know how they would feel about me. Her mother was very welcoming straight away, but her father treated me with suspicion and distanced himself from me with his silence until after about 45 minutes when he went to his drink cabinet and returned with a bottle and two small glasses. That is when I knew that I had been accepted into the family. I had had a long day and they could see I was tired, they were probably tired too as it was quite late, so Branka showed me to where I would be sleeping, before leaving. She said that it was Ivana's bed. There was a crib there too. As I lay in bed I reflected on my turbulent day that had begun with blind panic in Budapest and continued with despair when I thought I had lost Ivana to the man in the leather jacket, relief when I discovered I hadn't, shock when I was told that I had become a father, total joy at seeing Ivana and my son and finally ended with me meeting my new family. The next morning it had stopped raining, and it really did feel like a new day. Ivana's father was not at home, but her mother made me feel at home. She didn't speak any English, but we communicated quite well. She phoned

167

Branka who told me that we would be bringing Ivana and the baby home that day. I had actually understood that from her mother. Picking my son up from the hospital was a proud moment and during the two weeks I spent there I bonded with him and got to know Ivana even more, convincing me that I really did want to marry her. I proposed to her three days ago and she accepted. It was only then that I phoned my parents to give them all the good news. So, I have been to Bratislava twice; the first time to meet my future wife, and the second time to meet my son. I still don't know where we will live, but we will have to decide before the start of next semester."

As they approached Budapest, Daniel asked Tom where he was staying and recommended a dormitory he knew to be inexpensive and easy to find.

At the station, Tom wished Daniel all the best with his new life and set off to find the dormitory. It wasn't long before he had found and checked into the dormitory where he would possibly share the room with several other people. There was no one in the room when he walked into it, with four beds to choose from, but soon after he had lain on one of the beds closest to the window the door opened and a slim man with brown hair and a short beard walked in with a green haversack on his back. He introduced himself as Philippe while extending a hand in Tom's direction and placed his haversack near one of the vacant beds. He said that he was from Belgium and had never been to Hungary before, though he had travelled extensively even as far as Japan and India where he had been several times.

"I still haven't been to Budapest," he said. "With that thing on my back, I'm just a tourist. And that's how people see me. They behave differently in front of me. But when

I blend in with the locals, I can see how they live and feel how they feel."

"How do you blend in with the locals?" asked Tom.

"You have to notice how much eye contact they make and for exactly how long, how much space they need, whether or not they smile and how they walk. You have to mimic their facial expressions and everything else. I will become Hungarian in a day. Of course, I will pick up some of the language too."

Tom said that he would like to see that, and Philippe said that he could follow him discreetly from a distance. The area where the dormitory was situated was not overcrowded, but Philippe managed to walk closely behind several Hungarians without being noticed. He then casually walked around until he came to a kiosk where he stood looking and then casually walked away just as the salesman was about to open his mouth. He later said, "I left letting the man think I was Hungarian."

Tom had followed Philippe for about half an hour and seen enough, so he closed the gap until his presence was acknowledged and the two were reunited. As they walked around Philippe noticed a small restaurant that he said would not normally attract tourists and thought it would be cheap and a good place to eat like a native. He looked at the menu and ordered in Hungarian, though he was not sure what he was ordering, while Tom noticed that there was a section in English, so he pointed to the corresponding item in the Hungarian section with confidence. The restaurant wasn't far from where they were staying, but the night was young, so they bought some ice cream and sat by the Danube to take in the splendour of Budapest. Philippe said that he would spend another day in Budapest before going to Lake Balaton and after that, he would either go to India where he could live cheaply or to Scandinavia where he had never been before. As they were talking Tom noticed a girl with long blond hair and big blue eyes wearing a pink dress, who stood out like a pink rosebush in the desert. He recognised her instantly, even though he knew he had never met her before. He remembered several years earlier back in England he had been to the seaside with some friends where a fortune-teller had given him a reading telling him that he would meet and marry a foreign girl with long blond hair. Since then, he had met quite a few girls with those descriptions, but had never given that woman's prophecy a second thought. Suddenly her words came flooding back and he got a strong feeling that he was looking at his future wife. As he rose, he indicated to Philippe with his trailing hand that he should remain seated while he went to talk to the blonde girl in pink. She reacted to Tom's approach in a friendly manner as if she had been expecting him. She said that she was Sinikka from Finland and was travelling with her sister who had dashed back to where they had been sitting to see if she had left her cardigan there. Moments later a girl with short blond hair walked rapidly towards them with a broad smile on her face and a yellow cardigan in her hand. After a short introduction, Sinikka said that they were meeting a Hungarian family for a meal and were running late but said that they would be going to a place called Siofok by Lake Balaton the next day and to her sister's surprise asked Tom if he would like to join them. Tom said that he was going to Zagreb the next day as he had less than a week to get back to England but suggested that they met at the station and travelled together, as Siofok was on the way to Zagreb. Sinikka thought it was a brilliant idea. Tom said that they should exchange addresses to be on the safe side. The girls then rushed off to dine with their Hungarian hosts while

Tom returned to Philippe and explained what had just happened. Philippe said that he had met several people in India who had claimed to have psychic powers.

He said, "When I was in Mumbai, I got talking to a man who told me that I would one day meet my long-lost brother. I laughed and told him that I was an only child. He said that in fact I was a twin, and that my parents had given my brother up for adoption when he was only a few weeks old. A week later I was in Goa when another man told me the same story and said that for a fee, he would tell me where to find my long-lost brother. I thought if there was any truth in the story, I should ask my parents, so I refused to pay him anything and said that I was not interested. When I was leaving Goa I met an American man who was excited because he said that he was going back home to meet his twin brother he had never met before after two psychic men on different occasions and in different cities had told him about his existence. He said that after paying the second man, he was told that he would find his brother on a bridge where the sun sets between two towers."

Tom was still willing to believe what that woman had told him about his future wife could be true. Sinikka had been very friendly considering he was a total stranger and had seemed very keen to meet him again, so perhaps it really was destiny written in the stars, Tom thought. That night at the dormitory, Tom and Philippe shared the room with another person who was already asleep when they got there.

Day 26 Friday

When Tom woke up in the morning, Philippe was already up, and about to leave the room. He had said that he was an early riser and liked to be up and about when people were on their way to work. It wasn't long before Tom left the room too, checking to make sure he hadn't left anything behind without waking his sleeping roommate. After making inquiries at the reception desk, Tom took the underground to a modern shopping centre where he bought some food for breakfast and looked around in some of the shops before exploring Budapest a bit more on his way to the station. At the station, Tom waited nervously for Sinikka, until it was time to board the train. He chose a seat, reserved it with the bag of food he had bought on the way to the station, and stood by the door with a watchful eye in anticipation, but finally as the train began to chug out of the station he returned to his seat with great disappointment and began to eat some of the food, accepting that perhaps it just wasn't meant to be. After his late breakfast, Tom walked the length of the train to see if Sinikka had somehow got on the train without him noticing. When he returned to his seat, he saw that a man with dark brown hair and a moustache, wearing stripy trousers and a black shirt, had removed the bag with what was left of his food and taken his window seat. He looked at the man and then at his bag of food before taking the vacant seat. The man immediately stood up, said something in Hungarian, and offered Tom his seat. Tom said it was OK, but the man apologised in English and insisted that Tom should take the window seat.

He said, "I have travelled this route many times and don't need to look out of the window anymore. Two years ago, I was travelling to Lake Balaton with two of my friends when we met a man who said that he worked for a property development company and was building villas by the lake. He started to complain about his job saying that people sometimes ask him to build something but then pull out due to lack of money. He said that he had a property that was almost finished and asked if we would like to invest. It was a big house that would be quite expensive, but he said that he could give us a good deal. We said that we were university students one year before graduation and didn't have that kind of money. The man smiled and said that he was confident he would sell it within one week of advertising it. He told us about some of the sales he had made and suddenly said that he had a great idea. He suggested that we could pay a small amount for him to start building a villa that would be ready by the time we graduated, when we would pay the remainder at a reduced price. When we got off the train, he showed us some villas that his company had built and took us to a building site where he showed us a plot of land and said they could build us a villa there. He told us that he would be on the same train exactly a week later, so if we were interested, we could meet him half an hour before departure with 5% of the cost of the villa, and he would pay for our tickets to take us to the site, where we would choose the exact location. Two weeks later we would meet him at the site for an inspection and another payment of 5%, and the final payment would be 70% a year later, leaving us with a 20% discount. He said that we could even sell the villa before we had made the final payment and pay him with the proceeds, keeping the profits to ourselves. One of my friends was very excited by his offer, and a week later, after a lot of thinking and financial planning, we were at the station with a cheque for the agreed sum. The man arrived late and said that we should go to his office to sign the contract before he could take any money from us, but then he changed his mind and said that there wouldn't be enough time and we could sign the contract and pay after choosing our plot of land, otherwise we would miss the train. He bought us our train tickets as he had promised and we took our seats on the train, but he said that it was a big day for us and we probably wanted to be alone and that he would join us when we reached our destination. He was right; we were pretty excited at the prospect of becoming property owners. When we got off the train, we realised why he had been keen to go off on his own; he had used the time to find another potential buyer. He joined us with a short man who had dark curly hair and fat legs, telling us that he was interested in seeing the villas. He left the man to look at the villas and took us to where the new villas were to be built. An hour later, we had chosen the exact location of the villa and paid our first deposit. He didn't accept our cheque and said that we should go to the bank together and transfer the money into an account number he had given us.

"Two weeks later, we met him at the site and were happy to see that they had begun to build our villa. After receiving the rest of the deposit, the man told us that we could inspect the villa at any time and contact him at his office if there was anything we didn't like. As we were all students, we didn't have time to go to see the villa that often, but in nine months I had been there four times, and my friends had also been there and seen how much progress was being made. The day after our graduation we all went to see if the villa had been finished and were delighted with what we saw, but when we got closer, we

174

noticed that there were some people barbequing in the garden. We walked into the garden and asked them what they were doing on our property and were about to walk into the villa when they stopped us and said that it was their villa and that we should leave. We told them that if they didn't leave, we would call the police, but they told us that they had rented the villa and that it was theirs until the end of the following week. When we said that the agency did not have our permission to rent the villa, they said that they had rented it from a short man with curly hair who had taken the rent and given them the keys. They told us that he was a local man, and that one of them could take us to confront him. We walked furiously with the tenant and asked around until we finally came face to face with the man working in a shop. He was the short man we had seen getting off the train with the man who had sold us the villa.

"He said, "I remember you from the train; you went off with the man I had been talking to, who showed me some villas and asked me to look around while he conducted some business with you. I didn't wait for him but a few days later I returned to the site and contacted the company that was building the villas. They said that they had never heard of the man I had spoken with, but showed me where they were going to build their next villa and we agreed on a price. I think the man I met on the train was a con artist, who thought that I was a visitor and wouldn't be spending much time here, but I have a shop here and know the local businesses quite well. If he has taken your money you should go to the police. I will help if you need me to testify."

"We were feeling very down and went straight to the police. They asked us a lot of questions and we were able to give them a lot of important information. About a month later the police told us that they had arrested the man who had taken money from a lot of people. We got our money back plus an award for helping bring him to justice. We had been saving everything we could during our last year at university and now that we are all working, we were able to take out a mortgage and buy a villa. I make money by renting the villa and as I have moved back with my parents, I hope to soon be able to buy a flat in Budapest. The short shopkeeper sometimes sends customers our way when he gets too many replies to his ads, so we are doing well. When the villa is empty my friends and I like to go there to relax. We are happy that this happened to us because now we have our own villa."

The station where the happy Hungarian villa owner got off was small but quite crowded with tourists and families vying to board the train. Just as Tom reached for his bag to finish off the food he had purchased from Budapest, two children - a boy and a girl - pounced on the vacant seats near where Tom was sitting and began poking each other until their mother, carrying one rather large bag and a much smaller one, arrived and brought them under control. Tom rose to help the woman place her bag on the overhead rack but was only needed for the final push making sure it was securely in place. The young mother with fairly long brown hair who was wearing an above knee-length yellow dress thanked Tom before attending to her children giving them snacks, which made him feel less guilty about eating in front of them. After eating, the family engaged in a word game where to Tom's surprise English words seemed to be the answer.

Noticing Tom's quizzical look and then smile of approval, the woman explained, "I'm an English teacher back home in Croatia and would like the twins to speak English, so I have been teaching them a few words and sentences while their father who is a musician keeps their

176

musical interests alive. They start school this year and already know a bit of English and can play the piano."

After a bit of encouragement, the children said a few things in English and were able to understand Tom's easy questions, but their English knowledge was soon exhausted and they switched back to Croatian though they continued to include Tom in their fun and games. By the time they arrived in Zagreb Tom had built a rapport with the family and got invited to stay with them for the night. The mother, whose name was Katarina, took her two children and led Tom to her car that was parked a few streets away from the station and after driving through the streets of Zagreb, which captured Tom's interest, drove into the driveway of a house and welcomed Tom in. He was shown to a large living room while the children ran upstairs yelling something in Croatian. Katarina poured them all some orange juice and called the twins to come down and join them. Tom had finished his juice and was looking at an English book they had brought down when the doorbell rang and Katarina went to open the door. A man's voice was greeted by screams from the twins, who ran excitedly to the door, and after a short conversation, went upstairs and sounded very busy opening and closing cupboard doors. Katarina returned to the living room and explained that her estranged husband had come to pick up the twins as he does every weekend.

She said, "I thought we had agreed that, as we had been away, he would pick them up tomorrow. They were excited that you are staying here, but they do love their father and enjoy spending time with him."

As the children came down with their bags and kissed their mother goodbye, Tom noticed a tallish man wearing black jeans and a black t-shirt with a brown fringe peer into the living room as his children ran towards him. With the

177

children gone Katarina turned to Tom and said, "This might sound selfish, but being separated means that I can get some quality time to myself for reading or meeting friends. Otherwise, the television would be on the whole time and there wouldn't be a moment's peace. Of course, by Sunday evening I have had enough time by myself and look forward to seeing my children again. I think this has made us closer. It's just nice to be able to stay in bed a bit longer on weekends. Talking of beds, we don't have any spare ones, so you will have to sleep on the sofa. And I just remembered, we don't have much food either. You must be hungry; I know I am. We should have gone shopping on our way back, but we can go now."

At that moment a car skidded into the driveway and a few seconds later the doorbell began to ring furiously. Katarina rushed to the door and opened it. Tom heard the voice of her husband talking rapidly in desperation, and for the first time wished that he had been given the choice to take Croatian instead of Woodwork at school. Katarina seemed to be trying to calm him down, and soon they were both speaking gently but sounded emotional. The man quietly left the house and Katarina returned to the living room with tears in her eyes, looked at Tom and said, "It was my husband; he said that seeing you here made him madly jealous, and he realised that he couldn't spend a moment longer without me. When I told him that you were just a guest, he was so relieved that he began to cry. I had never seen him like that before and it made me love him even more. We decided to end our separation and continue our marriage."

Just then the children walked in and went upstairs to their room in a state of confusion. The husband closed the front door behind him and walked into the living room and spoke with his wife in Croatian. After a few minutes,

Katarina turned to Tom and said, "We appreciate what you have done for us, but we would like to be alone. Niko will get some pizza and take you to stay with a friend of his."

Her husband then called the children who rushed down excitedly when they heard the word pizza and after saying goodbye to Katarina, Tom sat in the car with Niko and the children. Katarina said that her husband spoke no English and asked Tom what kind of pizza he would like. They all went into the pizzeria and shortly returned with several boxes of pizza. Niko drove to a grey building and rang the doorbell while Tom waited in the car. After a short conversation, a man with a ginger beard and hair tied back tightly approached Tom and introduced himself as Dragan, while Niko took Tom's haversack from the boot of the car, handed it to him with an apologetic expression, and said, "Sorry!" From the look of lust in his eyes, Tom could see that he wasn't sorry and just couldn't wait to get back to Katarina. Tom waved to the children and followed Dragan into the dimly lit grey concrete house, luggage on back and pizza in hand, feeling that he had been forced to accept a downgrade, but at the same time, looking forward to spending the evening in the company of a singleton. There was a coffee table and some cushions on the floor, but a rather grand-looking drum set stood out in a living room that Tom noticed did not even have a television. Dragan invited Tom to sit on one of the cushions on the floor, saying that he preferred to be close to the earth. Tom offered a share of his pizza, but Dragan said that he had just eaten and returned from the kitchen with some cold beer and two clean glasses.

"So how did you meet Katarina?" asked Dragan. Tom told him about his train trip and how the twins had wanted him to stay with them.

"Nikolai and Nikolina are great kids," said Dragan. "Niko loves them very much but hasn't been around as much as he would like to. When they were born, he almost quit the band, but we persuaded him to stay on by agreeing to change our schedule. After a while, things got back to normal and he began to spend less time with his wife and kids. When they separated, he took the kids every weekend, but they didn't stay with him. He would take them to stay with his parents because he didn't have a place of his own. He often stayed with me or other members of the band. I guess he always believed he would get back with Katarina. We often had gigs at the weekend, but he would still take his children to fun places in the daytime. Talking of weekends, I never stay in at weekends; there's a party tonight, you can come with me if you want."

It was already quite late when they got into Dragan's old-fashioned Volkswagen and drove to a large house on the outskirts of Zagreb where Dragan got out of the car and gave his car keys and some money to a man who parked it neatly beside a fleet of cars in a field next to the house. Tom was both impressed and surprised at the service they had received, but Dragan explained that it was just a gimmick to welcome the guests who wanted to pay something towards the drinks. He said that most of the guests were in the music business or actors and some of them were quite rich.

Tom and Dragan walked round the building and through the large patio doors, which had been left open not only for the guests but also for the smoke some of them were exhaling, into a spacious room with several large settees and matching armchairs being occupied by groups of people engaged in conversation, while others were standing in small clusters with their drinks. As Dragan entered, he was greeted by several people who seemed very interested when he told them that Tom was visiting from England, and were eager to talk to him about the nightlife and celebrities in London. Tom was happy to talk with anyone who was interested, especially the girls who were very friendly, and was not too thrilled when a thin man wearing a suit and a long narrow tie barged in and began to impose himself on the conversation. Tom guessed that he was intoxicated by more than just alcohol and was glad to eventually see the back of him, but by that time the girls had left too. There was a bar at the other side of the room where Dragan had poured himself a drink and was talking with two other men but stopped talking and beckoned Tom over offering him a drink when he saw him standing alone. He recommended a drink that he described as a Croatian brandy, which tasted quite fruity and met with Tom's approval. Tom tried several drinks and began to feel that he was in charge of the bar even pouring drinks for some of the other guests, though he didn't really know what he was doing.

The volume increase of the background music prompted several couples to move to the centre of the room to the rhythm of the music, but Tom was happy to continue drinking, until he noticed a beautiful girl with long blond hair sitting in an armchair wearing a short black dress and decided that it was time to dance. He had only taken one step when she rose to her feet, but before Tom could rue his missed chance, she walked straight towards him and without saying a word, with a gentle smile and seductive look invited him to dance. They soon melted into each other's arms and before long were kissing unaware of their surroundings. While fast songs were being played, they took a break for more drinks and a chat. She said that her name was Malena and told Tom that she felt something special when she was with him; something she just

181

couldn't explain. Next time the slow music started, they didn't bother going to the centre of the room but just embraced where they were and began to kiss passionately.

Day 27 Saturday

It was just gone nine in the morning when Tom woke up with a headache, alone and fully clothed on a bed in a room he could not recall seeing before. His shoes were on the floor several metres apart and after remembering that he had gone there with Dragan and met Malena, he put his shoes on still trying to remember how he had got to the room. He quietly left the room and began to look for any sign of life. The patio door was now closed and there was no one in the living room. The bar seemed much less tempting, but he noticed a kitchen he hadn't seen before and helped himself to some food that lay on the table from the previous night. From the kitchen window, Tom could see the field where Dragan's car had been parked and noticed that it was not there. If Dragan had left without him, Tom would be without his luggage and passport until they were somehow reunited, so he started looking for him peeping into rooms where he saw several people sleeping, but there was no sign of Dragan. Hoping that Dragan was behind one of the closed doors, Tom returned to the kitchen where he was soon joined by a sleepy man who straightaway began rummaging in the cupboard for coffee ignoring Tom until he was asked about Dragan's whereabouts. He said that he was most probably sleeping in one of the rooms and when Tom told him that his car was missing, he took him to the front of the building where Dragan's car was parked alongside four other cars. At least Tom was now confident that Dragan was somewhere in the building, but it was a matter of getting back to his place and to the station in time for the 12:30 train to Maribor. The guests who had spent the night there were gradually waking up and finding something to drink and eat in the kitchen before leaving. Tom asked the guests about the whereabouts of Malena, but no one knew whom he was talking about. It was gone 10 o'clock when one of the guests left, only to return moments later and Tom understood that he had been unable to get his car out of the driveway. His car had been blocked by another car, so he went to find the owner and to Tom's relief, it was Dragan who came back with him keys in hand. After moving his car, Dragan poured himself a cup of coffee and sat down drinking it slowly while Tom nervously looked at his watch. Finally, just before 11 o'clock, Dragan was ready to leave. In the car, Tom asked about Malena, but Dragan said that he didn't know anyone by that name. Tom described her in detail, but Dragan said, "I know everyone who was there, and there was no such person." He could not understand how Dragan had not noticed him dancing with Malena and felt rather confused. Tom picked his belongings up from Dragan's house and was driven to the station just in time to board the train to Maribor, but as the train left the station, he had a strong feeling that he was leaving something behind. He had seriously considered getting off the train to try and find Malena, but he wouldn't know where to start as he was pretty sure he would be unable to find Niko, Dragan or the place he had spent the previous night. Suffering from a headache since the morning, Tom took a couple of painkillers, asked a girl who was sitting nearby if she would wake him up before Zidani Most and made himself as comfortable as possible before dozing off. A couple of taps on the arm woke Tom, who was feeling much better, as the girl pointed to the sign at the station while gathering her belongings. It was a small station running alongside a river surrounded by green mountains.

"You must have been tired," the girls said as they stepped onto the platform.

Tom explained that he had spent the night partying with Croatian celebrities he had never heard of and said that he was no longer tired but would like to find a place to buy some food during the one hour that he had to wait for the connecting train to Maribor. The girl, who was wearing purple trousers and a woollen sweater that seemed too warm for that time of year, said that she too was going to Maribor and followed Tom in search of a shop. In the shop, she said that it was nice to go shopping together just like a married couple and began talking about having children together, which made Tom feel uncomfortable. On the way back to the station she told Tom that she was the jealous type and would not let him out of her sight. Tom had not shaved since Budapest so at the station he asked the girl to wait for him on the platform while he went to the Gents for a shave. While shaving he tried to think of ways to get on the train unnoticed, but he knew the girl would be waiting for him on the platform and just telling her to go away would not help. When he left the Gents', Tom saw a girl and called her in desperation. Explaining what had happened, he asked if she would join him on the platform a few minutes later if he was still with that girl and pretend to be his girlfriend. She asked his name and said that her name was Lara and would be on the platform after three minutes. Tom walked onto the platform with more confidence and when the girl approached him said that he had appreciated her company but would like to be alone because he was waiting for his girlfriend, who was very jealous.

The girl said, "Don't worry my darling, I am here. You have already found me."

At that moment Lara called out Tom's name and he rushed to her with a genuine-looking smile. Lara had shoulder-length brown hair and a shapely figure accentuated by her snugly fit burgundy corduroy trousers and tight t-shirt. She said that she was Austrian and on her way home to Graz. It was then that Tom realised that she was waiting for a different train and would not be travelling with him, making way for the girl in the purple trousers, so he suggested that instead of waiting another hour to take the direct train she could travel with him and change at Maribor. She said that it was a good idea and got on the train with him.

"I've had a strange day," she sighed as they took their seats. "I had been travelling with my friend Regina and it was our last day today. We were taking the early train from Zagreb to Graz and found ourselves in a bit of a rush to catch the train. As we walked into the station, we knew that we would have to run to our train. We were relieved to get on the train and find good seats, but luckily before the train had moved, we found out that we were on the wrong train. Regina still had her rucksack on her back and ran off the train just in time to jump on the correct train, but I had already put my things on the rack and by the time I managed to get off the train, the other train was leaving with Regina on it. She called out through the train window and said that she would look out for me on the next train. I had to wait for five hours and then change trains at Zidani Most where I was hoping she might be waiting for me. On the train from Zagreb, I was talking to two Finnish girls and now when you suggested that we could travel together I thought it would be nice to have someone to take my mind off Regina so that I don't worry that I might have already passed her."

As they were talking, Tom noticed the girl with the purple trousers had appeared from out of nowhere with a pair of scissors and was about to cut a chunk out of Lara's hair. He just managed to push her hand away and saved Lara from having an even worse day. The girl started to shout in her native language and some of the passengers who spoke the same language started to shout back at her, making so much noise that the conductor had to intervene and take her away. At the next stop, the girl was put off the train and an unpleasant situation turned into a mere talking point. The rest of the journey passed without incident and was quite pleasant, with Tom and Lara able to relax and get to know each other better. When they got off the train at Maribor station, Lara screeched and ran towards a girl who could only have been Regina. As Tom joined them, Lara said with a smile that he was her boyfriend and he had rescued her from baldness. She then explained what had happened and thanked Tom for suggesting that they should change at Maribor where unbeknownst to him Regina was waiting. Regina said that she had intended to get off at Zidani Most, but had fallen asleep and was, in fact, glad that she hadn't had to spend so many hours in such a small place. Tom only spent a short time with the two friends, who seemed to enjoy his company, as he wanted to see as much as Maribor as possible, rather than waste an hour at the railway station. Lara told Tom that she would be happy to show him her hometown if he arrived on the morning train the next day, and Tom said that he would be on that train. It had been a warm day, and as Tom walked around looking for affordable accommodation, he was drawn to a small restaurant where he splashed out on a meal and a cold beer before relaxing by the river, planning his next move. Putting up his tent seemed like an appealing idea if he could find a secluded spot by the river, but he would have to wait until nightfall. Tom began to walk along the river, watching passers-by and looking for the perfect place to pitch his tent until he noticed a girl with straight brown hair wearing a light floral dress who was reading a London guidebook. His curiosity got the better of him and he asked her why she was reading a London guidebook in Maribor. She said that she was going to London the next day and began to ask Tom questions about places to see and things to do in London. She said that her name was Mara and that she had always been interested in England and the English language.

"Until a few weeks ago, going to England was just something I had always wanted to do," she said, "About a year ago my mother began getting headaches that became more and more frequent, but being a workaholic, she refused to take time off to see her doctor. Her eyesight was suffering too, but she continued to work as hard as ever. One day she narrowly missed a collision with a lorry. I was in the car with her, and we were both quite shaken. She admitted that her eyesight was to blame and finally agreed to seek medical help. Her doctor carried out some tests and sent her for a brain scan. The day she went for the result she was very nervous and asked me to go with her. We arrived half an hour early but within five minutes my mother was called in. I had just had enough time to go to the ladies' room and was surprised on my return to see my mother slowly making her way to the doctor's room while looking for me. It wasn't her usual doctor, but before my mother could say anything, she introduced herself and said that my mother's usual doctor had moved to another district and that she would be taking over some of her patients. She asked us to sit down and then told us, while pointing to a negative on the wall, that they had found an incurable brain tumour. She said that my mother would

188

have about one year to live. We looked at each other in disbelief and simultaneously burst into tears. When we left, I was holding my mother and she was visibly shaking. We took a taxi home as neither of us felt that we could drive. That was by far the worst day of my life. I spent the next days in a daze, but my mother continued working until the beginning of the following week when her headaches got worse, and she finally told her boss and was put on sick leave.

"She decided to take things easy and do things that she enjoyed doing. We went ice-skating together, went to the theatre to see a play, and she contacted friends she had not seen for many years. She even took up meditation which made her much calmer. We spent quality time together as a family and I could see that she was beginning to enjoy life again and even getting fewer headaches.

"One day my mother received a letter from the health centre asking why she had not kept her appointment with her doctor and offered her another appointment. She phoned and told them that she had already been seen, but they said that they had no record of her visit and gave her another appointment. When she arrived, to her surprise, she was seen by her regular doctor who knew nothing about her brain tumour and told her that her headaches had been caused by stress which had also affected her eyesight. It transpired that a person with a similar name to my mother had had an appointment half an hour before her, but she had been taken ill and was in hospital. When they called her name, my mother who was feeling very stressed and nervous thought they were calling her and walked in. The doctor had never met my mother or the woman with the tumour whose doctor she was replacing. That is how the misunderstanding happened.

"When my mother arrived home, she looked like a new person. She couldn't wait to break the news to us. I couldn't believe it. I hugged her as hard as I could and once again burst into tears. But this time it was tears of happiness. I decided to celebrate my mother's life and show how much I loved her, by buying tickets for us to travel to London together. I had been saving up and had just enough money for the tickets, but when my father heard what I had decided to do, he said that it would be a nice gesture for me to pay for my mother's ticket but offered to pay for my ticket and gave me spending money too. My mother handed in her resignation at work, but they didn't want to lose her, so they offered her a month's vacation with pay and a promotion on her return with much better working conditions."

Tom gave Mara his phone number and said that she could phone him anytime after Wednesday and he would show her and her mother around London. Mara said that if they had had more time, she could have taken him swimming at a swimming pool on an island in Maribor she liked to frequent. When Tom mentioned that he was thinking of camping somewhere Mara said that he could probably stay with her cousin as his roommate was away at the time. She phoned her cousin and confirmed that it would be OK for Tom to stay with him. After walking around a bit and showing Tom parts of Maribor that were within walking distance, Mara said that she had to go home and pack for her trip to London. Tom set off to find Mara's cousin with the directions she had given him, and just as he was about to ask a local for the correct entrance to the building, he heard his name being called. It was Mara's cousin Zlatko calling from his window, telling him how to get upstairs.

Zlatko was thin with dark hair, who was soon joined by a short fidgety young man who walked into the room with a six-pack of local beer and immediately shook hands with Tom and said, "Hi, my name's Kurt. Do you believe in aliens?" Tom didn't know what to say and before he had time to say anything Kurt continued, "I believe that the aliens are coming to visit us. They will come within five years from now and will land in Buckingham Palace. I believe they pick up our television signals in space and because there are so many films in English, they speak English better than any other language. They would not want to land in America in case they got shot, so they would choose England and the best place would be Buckingham Palace where they would be out of the reach of the public, but in full view of the Royal Family who people trust. Once they had been witnessed by the Royal Family and brought to the attention of the world, by watching our television, the aliens would know how people feel about them and could plan where to land so that they can make contact and communicate with people."

Kurt was very excited that Tom was from England, the landing place of the aliens, but Zlatko wanted to spare Tom, so he changed the subject and started to talk about football, which was not something Kurt had much interest in and was unable to keep up with the conversation. Having conveyed his message, it wasn't long before Kurt finished off his beer, grasped Tom's hand with a serious look, gave it one shake and a nod of the head, and walked out without a word.

Zlatko said, "You made his day by listening to his theory. His real name isn't Kurt; we have given him that name because he looks like a mole. He seems to like it."

Tom and Zlatko briefly contemplated going out to catch some of the nightlife but decided against it, as Tom wanted to leave early to catch the morning train to Graz.

Day 28 Sunday

Tom slept like a log and woke up full of energy and ready to go, which he did after a quick shower and shave, and having bread, butter and honey with tea for breakfast. Zlatko joined Tom for breakfast, but it was obvious that he intended to go straight back to bed for a Sunday sleep-in as soon as he was alone.

Tom had overestimated how long it would take to get to the station and arrived with plenty of time to spare, but there was not much to do or see at the station, so he went straight to the platform and waited for the train. There were already some people waiting on the platform, and Tom got talking to a man wearing a light brown shirt and dark brown jeans with circular spectacles who didn't look like the rest of the crowd, as he was only carrying a very small bag. He said that he was Hans and was on his way back to Vienna. When the train arrived, Tom and Hans sat next to each other to continue their conversation. Hans said that he was a frequent traveller to Maribor.

"Last year, I went to the Munich beer festival for the first time. I had heard a lot about it but had never been there, so some friends and I decided to spend a few days there. I can tell you that we had a lot of beer and a great time. On the second day, I met a girl who was just out of this world. Well, she was from Slovenia, to be precise. We shared a lot of interests, and I ended up abandoning my friends and spending the rest of my time in Munich with her. She was working in a company in Munich doing the same kind of work that I was doing back home. Even on the train back, I was not really with my friends as I was daydreaming about her. The following weekend she came to visit me in Vienna, and it was then that I decided to see if there were any vacancies at the company in Munich where she was working. I didn't tell her of my plan in case I didn't get the job. I thought it would be a nice surprise for her if I suddenly turned up at her workplace and announced that I was her new work colleague. I contacted the company and was told that I could apply for the job. A week later, I was called for an interview and was straight away told that I could start at the beginning of the following month, giving me enough time to resign from my job in Vienna. I was so excited that I knew I would not be able to keep the secret from her if I saw her or spoke with her for more than a few minutes, so I told her that I would be going away on business and would contact her when I returned. I had just bought my flat in Vienna, so I decided to rent it out and find rented accommodation for myself in Munich. I had to do all this in just over a week, so it was hectic. But on the first day of the month, I reported for work in Munich. I was very nervous. Not so much because of my new job, but because I knew how surprised and happy she would be to see me. I imagined I would bump into her as soon as I walked into the building, or at least within the first 30 minutes. After several hours my excitement had diminished and I was concentrating on my work, and by the end of the day, I was feeling rather disappointed. I could only think that she had taken the day off, so when I didn't see her the next day, I asked around and was told that she was no longer working there. I felt like banging my head against the wall when I found out that she had been in a trial period and had been refused a permanent contract because according to them I was more qualified. I think it was because German was my first language, and I had more experience than her. I went to her flat, but it was too late; she had already moved out and returned to Maribor. I had given up a lot to be with her, but she had lost even more as a result of it and couldn't even talk to me about her job loss and next move, as I had told her that I could not be contacted. When I spoke with her on the phone, I didn't tell her what had happened or where I was. I just said that I would like to visit her in Maribor. And that is where I told her the whole story. She said that it had been a romantic gesture and didn't resent my taking her job. I didn't blame the company in Munich for not giving her a contract, but I felt bad about working there. So, as I was still in my trial period, I told them that I would not be signing a contract with them and left.

When I was leaving my job in Vienna, they had offered me more money to stay, so before quitting my job in Munich, I asked them if the offer was still on the table, and they said that they would be happy to have me back. Since then we have been seeing each other as often as possible, but this was probably the last time I travel to Maribor because last week my boss, who knew why I initially left my job, said that there will be a vacancy at the company and asked if my girlfriend would be interested. This time when I went to Maribor, I told her about the job offer and asked her if she would like to move in with me, so it looks like we can finally be together."

Tom wished Hans luck as he got off the train at Graz station, where Lara was waiting. She took him to her car and was soon driving through the countryside. She explained that she had a flat in Vienna where she was working, but liked to go home to her mother and sisters as often as she could. Lara was a very fast driver, so Tom was relieved when she drove up a path and skidded to a halt outside a large house on a hill.

"I told my mother that you are my boyfriend," she said. "I pretended on the train and it was fun, so now I want to

195

see if I can fool someone who knows me. She will probably treat you better if she thinks you're my boyfriend."

Lara's mother was a roundish woman with a kind face, who greeted Tom nervously with a few well-chosen words in English that she had obviously rehearsed and seemed relieved to utter without an error. The sisters were much younger than Lara and couldn't—or didn't want to—speak any English. They promptly disappeared, having seen what they had come to see, giggling in the background.

Lara took Tom into the garden where, there was a table and two benches for them to sit. Her mother brought a jug of juice and two glasses and said, "Please!" Moments later, a large plate of strawberries appeared, which Lara explained were from the garden. She said that they would be having snacks and would be going down to the village later to join in the festivities. With the sun almost directly above them, Lara suggested that they should sit on the grass under her favourite cherry tree and take shelter until more snacks arrived. After helping themselves to a large bowl of potato salad with chicken, they returned to the cherry tree, where Tom fell asleep while Lara went in with the dishes. When Tom awoke from his short nap, he noticed that Lara was back in the garden reading a magazine, waiting for him to wake up. She immediately put the magazine down and asked if he would like to go for a walk. It was a big garden with no fence, but they soon came to a slope, at the bottom of which was another house. As they passed the house an unshaven middle-aged man appeared from behind it and exchanged a few sentences with Lara in German.

"My mother doesn't like me talking to that man," Lara told Tom as they walked away from the house.

"He used to live there with his wife, who was very popular in the community for her charity work and friendliness. He was quite a nice person too, often giving people lifts in his truck if they needed something heavy to be transported, though he was a bit quiet by nature. One night, we heard a lot of shouting from that house, and the next day she didn't turn up for a charity lunch she had promised to attend. Her husband said that she had to rush off to another town to see a friend who was very ill, but a few days later announced that she had been killed in a car accident on her way to see her friend. We were all shocked and wanted to know when the funeral would be, but he said that she would be cremated near Linz, where she had been brought up, and the ceremony was for family members only. I remember looking out of my bedroom window the night I heard the shouting, and seeing him digging in the garden at gone midnight. About nine months later, my sisters and I peeped into his garage that he always kept locked and saw his wife's car that was supposed to have been written off in the accident. My mother called the police anonymously, but they didn't do anything about it. When she phoned again a few days later to see what was being done, they thanked her and said that they were not allowed to discuss the case. We felt very uncomfortable living so close to that man, but about a year ago, I had been to Prague and stopped off in Linz on my way back, when I saw a woman, who at first glance looked very much like my neighbour's late wife, and on second glance looked exactly like her. I secretly took some pictures of her and confronted my neighbour. I know I should have discussed it with my mother first, but she was not at home, and curiosity did not allow me to wait for her. As soon as I mentioned that I had been to Linz, he knew what I wanted to talk about and became very emotional. He didn't want

197

to see the pictures I had taken, and told me that as far as he was concerned, the woman he had been married to no longer existed.

He said, "We met when we were very young, and I knew straight away that she was the only woman I would ever love. We were very happy together until one day her best friend from the village where she grew up fell ill and my wife, who was a qualified nurse, went to look after her. Luckily, she made a full recovery, but my wife was not the same anymore. She had met and fallen in love with a man she had known when they were children. She promised that nothing had happened between them but wanted a divorce. I pleaded with her to stay, as I could not imagine my life without her. One night when I came home, she had packed her essential belongings and said that she was leaving. I begged her to stay but she said that he was picking her up at the end of the street. As she left, I shouted out her name one last time, and even now, I think I can sometimes hear it echoing. That night I couldn't sleep, so I went into the garden and planted some of her favourite plants in her memory."

"He said that he was not only heartbroken but also felt inadequate as a man and would be embarrassed if anyone knew that he had lost his woman to another man. He swore me to secrecy.

"You are the only person I have ever told. I will never mention it to anyone who might know him or come into contact with him."

By that time, they had walked a full circle and were back beside the cherry tree. Lara said that they could freshen up before going to the festival, and a quarter of an hour later, Lara was driving down the bendy narrow path like a rally driver, making Tom wish he had eaten less chicken salad and taken out life insurance. She skidded into an open area where there were several cars already parked and got out of her car, followed by the trembling Tom. There was a marquee with tables and benches where beer and sausages were being consumed, with a band of four middle-aged lederhosen-clad men playing loud music. Further away from the band, where the music sounded more pleasant, there were stalls and minor activities, and by then Tom could see that Lara was well known by the locals, as she had been greeted by someone every few steps she had taken. She introduced Tom to a selected few, who made small talk with him before disappearing into the crowd. By the time they were returning to the marquee, Tom was bumping into people he had already met, and just as he was about to purchase his first Austrian beer, one of Lara's old classmates rushed over with a large glass of beer for him. As he was talking with Tom, Lara was drawn to a group of friends she hadn't yet greeted, and minutes later, when Tom looked, Lara was no longer there. As the music was quite loud, Tom left the marquee area only to see Lara drive off at full speed. He stood there wondering why she had left without saying anything and what might happen if she did not return. He walked around looking for Lara's friends, but suddenly they were few and far between, and those he asked had no idea where she had gone. After a lot of searching, he was once again near the marquee, where he recognised one of the girls Lara had been talking to, but just as he was about to approach her, he saw Lara get out of her car, walk towards the girl and hand her a book. At the same time, she noticed Tom and walked to him as if nothing had happened. When Tom asked why she had suddenly disappeared, she said that she had forgotten to bring a book she had borrowed from her friend and thought he was too preoccupied to notice her absence. Tom and Lara were joined by some of her friends as they sat down with Austrian sausages and beer, almost forgetting about the time until Lara remembered that she was giving Tom a lift to the station in Graz the next day to catch the eight o'clock train towards Liechtenstein. The speedy drive back through the narrow, bumpy road in the dark was a harrowing experience for Tom, whose head was still spinning a bit as he lay down for the night.

Day 29 Monday

Lara woke Tom up in the morning to say that he would have to get ready in a hurry and would not have time for breakfast, though she had put some food in a bag for him to have on the train. Her mother had just gone to bed after a night shift and her sisters were still asleep from the previous night, so they left quietly. Soon Tom was holding on tightly to his seat, counting his lucky stars that he had not yet eaten, while Lara raced towards Graz and the railway station, arriving just in time to find out that he would have to take a coach from just outside the station to Klagenfurt. Despite travelling over some rather flat terrain, the coach went through many tunnels, and each time two girls sitting behind Tom shrieked, "Oh no, is it night again?" laughed a bit and continued their serious conversation. Tom had some of the food Lara had packed for him and went through his book of train timetables to kill time until they reached Klagenfurt coach station, where he learned that he would have to walk to the train station. The two girls, who turned out to be from New Zealand, were also going to the railway station to catch the same train and asked Tom if he knew the way. Tom suggested that they follow some of the other passengers who seemed to know where they were going.

"Lots of tunnels," remarked Tom, hoping for some sort of explanation. After a few moments of silence, one of them opened up and said, "Last week, we were taking an overnight train and sharing our compartment with a Scottish woman and her young son. In the morning, when we woke up the woman gave her son some food she had in her bag, but the boy had only taken a few bites when the train entered a tunnel, and in the dark, we heard the boy say, 'Oh no, is it night again? ' Now, whenever we go into a tunnel, we think of that little boy."

The two girls were Kaz, who had black hair with glasses and was wearing jeans with a blue t-shirt, and Emily, who had long brown hair and was wearing stripy trousers and a grey t-shirt that had a lot of writing on it. The station was not far or difficult to find and the girls chose seats that were facing each other so that Tom could sit with them, or perhaps more legroom and a table was the main attraction. They said that they had flown from New Zealand into London, where they had spent eight days before travelling around Europe for two months and were going to fly out from Frankfurt the following Wednesday. They were on their way to Salzburg to stay with someone they had met when they were in Romania.

Kaz said, "While we were looking out of our youth hostel window, we noticed two men acting suspiciously. They were keeping an eye on who was coming out of the youth hostel, but didn't know that we could see them. That day, when we went shopping, we saw those two men in the supermarket targeting a female tourist we had seen at our hostel. We followed them discreetly and informed the security guard when we saw that one of them bumped into her and gave her purse to his accomplice. Both men were arrested, and we spent the next two days with the intended victim, who invited us to stay with her in Salzburg."

Emily said that they had learnt a lot about Europe and made lots of friends in the process, making it an unforgettable experience. By the time they reached their destination, they had added Tom to their list of friends and exchanged addresses with him.

Tom changed trains in Salzburg and chose a compartment occupied by a stern-looking man with a moustache, who was reading a newspaper, and a young girl with dark brown hair, wearing brown trousers and a beige blouse, eating a sandwich from a brown paper bag. He put his luggage on the rack above the girl's head and sat opposite her by the window. When she had finished eating, he asked her if she was an Interrailer.

"No," she replied. "I was visiting my grandparents in northern Austria for three weeks, and now I'm on my way back to Innsbruck. My aunt, who is not much older than me got, married and moved up there, so when she had her first child four years ago, my grandparents bought a small flat there to be close to their new grandchild. Since then, my aunt has had another child, and my grandparents enjoy living there very much, but they like to see me too, so they always pay for my tickets to go and stay with them. I live in their house in Innsbruck rent-free, which is nice."

She said that her name was Katrin and went on to talk about her university and asked Tom about his life back home and where he had been travelling.

As time passed, Tom felt hungrier and finally decided to reach out for the bag of food Lara had given him, to finish what he had left from breakfast. As soon as Tom began to eat, the stern-looking man folded his newspaper neatly, put it in his briefcase, and left.

Shortly after Tom had finished eating, the train pulled into a station, and Katrin said that she had reached her destination. She said goodbye to Tom, took her rucksack and several bags from the overhead rack, and left. Tom looked out of the window and saw her walking away on the platform, but just as she was about to disappear from view, he noticed a brown zipped-up bag on the rack next to his haversack and quickly grabbed, it calling out her name from the open window. The train began to move, so he swiftly handed the bag to a man on the platform and asked him to give it to the girl who had just stopped and turned around. Tom saw the man approach Katrin as the train gathered speed and thought how lucky she had been that he had noticed the bag in time and reacted quickly enough.

Moments later, the stern-looking man walked into the compartment with his briefcase in one hand and a cup of coffee in the other, sat down with his customary frown, and started to drink his coffee. Suddenly he rose to his feet and began shouting at Tom in German, pointing at the luggage rack. It was then that Tom realised that the bag he had handed to the man on the platform did not belong to Katrin, but he just shrugged his shoulders and pretended to be confused when a girl with wavy brown hair, carrying a sports bag, entered the compartment, asked the man what had happened, and translated his answer into perfect English. Tom, who could no longer hide behind his inability to speak German but did not want to own up to his mistake, quickly came up with a story and said, "I had just finished eating and had come back from washing my hands when I saw a man wearing light blue jeans and a black leather jacket rush out with a brown bag. The girl who was here had already left, and I hadn't seen that man before, so I shouted for him to be stopped. This made him run, but I saw a man catch him and take the bag from him. By this time the train had already started to move, and from what I could see, the bag was handed over to a guard on the platform. I'm sure the bag will be waiting for him at the station."

The girl translated what Tom had said, and when the conductor came to see the tickets, the man mentioned it to him. About 20 minutes later, the conductor returned to confirm that the bag had been handed in and would be forwarded to the station of his choice. The man nodded with gratitude, and the girl smiled at Tom and said, "I really admire you for what you did. Last year, when I was in Italy, I saw a man steal a tourist's purse from her handbag and did nothing about it. I suppose at the time I thought I might get into trouble. Even when she noticed that her purse was missing, I remained silent because I didn't want to be blamed for not saying anything in the first place. I felt guilty for a long time after it and still do when I think about it. You are a real hero. I wish there were more people like you." The girl continued to praise Tom's heroic action until he could take no more and finally admitted with reluctance, that it was he who had been responsible for the bag leaving the train. Before the girl could react, the man shouted in fairly good English but with a strong Austrian accent, "Why did you lie to me? It is your fault that my bag is lost. You are not a hero; you are dishonest."

Tom was shocked to hear the man speak English, but snapped back, "I was trying to be helpful and did what I thought was right. I could have said nothing, but my story helped you get your bag back, and I am no more dishonest than a man who pretends not to speak English."

The man went deep into thought and then left the compartment without uttering another word. It didn't take Tom, long to find out what the girl thought of him.

"It was very brave of you to stand up to him like that. And I think you are an honest enough person. If you hadn't been honest, you would have kept the bag for yourself, as you thought the girl who had left the train was the owner. And you are also very good at making up stories."

At the next station, the man put his head round the door and said, "Thank you!" with a hint of a smile and left the train. The girl got off at the stop after that and was replaced with a little round Swiss man and his slightly bigger and rounder Swiss wife, along with a pair of shy twin boys who constantly apologised for being alive. The slightest noise omitted by the twins, or any movement that was considered an invasion of personal space by them resulted in their extreme discomfort and feeling of shame. Tom was hoping to be left alone with the twins so that he could pretend to be poked in the eye by one of them, but soon warmed to the two chubby little boys and found himself trying to avoid any physical contact with them in case he embarrassed them. The father spoke enthusiastically of their interest in maths and their plan to take trombone lessons, while the mother was keen for Tom to sample her apple pie, which he gladly obliged.

Tom waited for over half an hour at Feldkirch for the train to Schaan Vaduz, from where he took a bus into Vaduz. It was already getting late, and Tom needed to find somewhere to stay, so he walked in the direction that the locals had told him he would find some hotels. The mountains and greenery that surrounded him made the walk an enjoyable experience, but the hotels were pricey, and he was not prepared to empty his bank account for the sake of a night's sleep, so as the rain began to fall, he turned around and headed towards the station. Within minutes, the rain was battering him relentlessly with no shelter in sight and only a small umbrella keeping both him and his luggage from getting totally soaked. About 30 minutes later, he was back at the bus station, where he saw an empty waiting room that seemed like a good place to spend the night. He was thinking that the wooden bench would be comfortable enough if his sleeping bag was still dry, when a girl with blond curly hair, wearing a tracksuit, walked in, looked at a timetable on the wall, and asked him where he was going. Tom said that he would be spending the night there and leaving the next morning for Italy, expressing regret that he would be unable to experience the mountains firsthand. The girl gave him some apples, wished him luck, and left, but around half an hour later, walked back into the waiting room and told Tom that her father had said he could stay at their place up in the mountains. She said that her name was Christine and took Tom to her father, who was waiting in his car. They drove up into the mountains until they reached a wooden house with a breathtaking view. Tom thought how wonderful it would be to live in such a remote place. As they passed an excited dog and entered the house, Christine's kid brother ran to the door and was prompted to say hello in English, while her mother, who had been cooking in the kitchen, greeted Tom and asked if he was hungry. Tom freshened up and was then called to the table, where they sat down for the meal that Christine's mother had been preparing. Later, Christine's mother asked her to collect any clothes Tom might need washing and put them in the washing machine. Christine's father said that he was the vice president of a large Swiss company and was very interested in what career path Tom was hoping to pursue, offering to take him to his workplace the next day. When Tom said that he had to leave the next day, he seemed quite surprised and said that he should definitely return and spend more time with them. By the time Tom was ready for bed, his laundry was washed and dry, and within minutes he had fallen asleep in a soft comfortable bed under a fluffy duvet, to the smell of fresh laundry and clean sheets.

Day 30 Tuesday

The next morning, Tom woke up to the sound of cowbells and noticed that it was still very early. He could hear movement in the house, and as he opened the curtains, he was struck by the beauty of dawn and thought it would be a waste to go back to sleep.

After his shower, Christine suggested that they go for a walk while her mother prepared breakfast. The fresh air and morning dew felt quite liberating as Tom and Christine walked up a path to a vantage point with her kid brother and dog on their trail.

"You remind my parents of my Uncle Thomas," Christine said with a slight snigger. "Even your name is like his. He used to travel a lot and enjoyed it very much, just like you do, until he reached New Zealand.

"He said that he was in Auckland on his way to the harbour to catch a ferry to a nearby island when an old lady staggered out of a shop and would have fallen to the ground had he not been able to catch her. He helped her to a bench where they sat for a while until he was sure that she could manage by herself and then walked her to her car and watched her drive off. As he walked towards the harbour, time was ticking away and the dark clouds that were gathering made it seem even later, which made him anxious and caused him to miss a turning. He asked a young jogger for directions, and she showed him the right way while jogging on the spot before speeding off as if to make up for lost time, which was more than my uncle could do. By the time he reached the harbour, it was too late and there wasn't a ferry leaving from that particular port until the next day. With nothing to do, he took the weight off his back and sat down planning his next few days. After resting and gathering his thoughts, he decided that before it started to rain, he should walk back towards the hostel he had spent the previous night to see if they had any beds left. He said that he hadn't gone far when a car slowed down next to him, and the driver called out in the cutest New Zealand accent, "So you didn't make the ferry then." It was the jogger girl having freshened up after her jog. He said that he jumped into her car before realising that she hadn't invited him. She looked at him without saying a word, which made him feel very awkward, but then to his relief, she smiled and asked him how long he had been in Auckland. She drove around showing him some of her favourite sights and they ate at a cosy little restaurant where they got to know each other. Time flew by and as it was probably too late for him to check into the hostel, she offered him a place on her couch. At least that's what he said. The next day, while he was taking a shower, she prepared breakfast and then drove him to the harbour, making sure he got there in good time. He said that as the ferry left the port, his heart sank, and he started to miss Wendy. He regretted leaving, but there was no turning back. At least not straight away. He had planned to spend several days on the island, but already after one day, he decided to return to Auckland. He said that he boarded the ferry with excitement though he wasn't sure he would remember how to get to Wendy's place from the harbour. He soon realized that the ferry was going to a different port in Auckland, which made his task even more difficult. He thought he could maybe find his way to the other port and try his luck from there, though he had no idea how far the other port was. He rushed off the ferry but soon slowed down to get his bearings, ignoring the people around him. Suddenly he felt a poke in his ribs, and when he turned round, to his amazement he saw the smiling face of Wendy. She told him that she had woken up in the morning with the strong feeling that he would be returning that day and somehow was drawn towards that particular port. Nine months later they were married. He met many of her friends and family for the first time at the wedding. Some had travelled from other cities to be there. He said that when he was briefly introduced to Wendy's grandmother, he felt that there was something different about her. He found himself spying on her from the corner of his eyes. After the ceremony, at the dinner table, several people made unmemorable speeches. But when the grandmother stood up and began to speak, he suddenly remembered that she was the old lady he had helped on the day he met Wendy. At the end of her short speech, she said, "They say that fate has brought these two young people together." She then paused and turned to my uncle with a piercing look and said with an eerie voice, "But I don't believe in fate." My uncle says that he still doesn't know if the grandmother remembers him from their first encounter and he hasn't mentioned it to anyone over there. I believe that when two people are meant to be together, they will find each other. Even if fate needs to be pushed in the right direction."

It suddenly occurred to Tom that perhaps he had been taken in because Christine's parents were hoping that a similar fate would befall their daughter, but then they were probably just being hospitable.

Christine said how she will miss all that nature when she starts university in Austria and asked Tom to visit her once she has settled in. They returned in time for breakfast with a healthy appetite brought on by the fresh air and brisk walk. When Tom was ready to leave, Christine's mother gave him several goodie bags full of chocolate, food and souvenirs; and even an envelope with some money for the journey which she insisted he took. Christine accompanied her father as he drove Tom down to the station across the border into Switzerland where he boarded the train to Milan.

Tom sat quietly enjoying the view until the train stopped at Zurich and a man with ginger hair wearing light blue jeans and a matching shirt got on the train and sat next to Tom after saying a few words in Italian. When Tom said that he only spoke English, the man's face lit up and he started to speak in a cockney accent admitting that he didn't speak Italian but had picked up a few phrases and was asking if the seat was free. He said that his name was Joe and that he had been travelling around Europe with his juggling act.

"I used to help my old man out at his fruit stall down the market," he said. "I started juggling fruit and found that I had a talent for it. People used to gather to see my bananas, which was trickier than your usual apples and pears. My old man didn't like me playing with the fruit, but when he saw that it brought in the crowds, he let me do it, as long as I used old fruit that we couldn't sell. I met this Italian kid called Fat Eddie who had a good pair of lungs on him and used to earn a few quid busking. He told me that I could make a bit of money on the side as a street entertainer, and I found that I really enjoyed it. I even entered competitions and won some cash prizes. Fat Eddie was good with the birds too; he could sing the pants off them. I was a chat-em-up kind of a guy and we had lots of laughs when we went out on the pull. One night we were down our local pub when Fat Eddie nudged me to draw my attention to some broad who'd just walked in. He went up to her and started singing, but she told him to shove off, so he came back with his tail between his legs. Fat Eddie

211

wasn't the kind of person to give up that easily, so he went back holding a bowl of salted peanuts in his hands. He said that the way he held the bowl mesmerised them and would have them eating out of the palm of his hand. A few minutes later they left the pub together; she in front and he following her behind with a bowl of salted peanuts, singing something by the Commodores. I thought he had pulled, but it wasn't long before he came back to the pub with a long face and spent the rest of the evening staring hopelessly at her empty seat, gently singing love songs. I didn't mind at first, but it started to feel weird when this middle-aged man wearing a suit sat where she had been sitting.

"Fat Eddie's brother, Luigi, did some detective work and found out that the woman was married to a Swiss banker but was having a fling with some geezer from Putney. He wrote anonymously to the husband informing him that his wife was seeing someone behind his back and two weeks later Fat Eddie disappeared. A day later the wife went missing too. After getting the letter, the husband had hired a private detective to follow his wife around to see if the information was true. The detective had taken pictures of her with Fat Eddie, who was still trying to seduce her, and mistook him for her lover. One night when Fat Eddie was walking home three men wearing tuxedos said that his girlfriend had a message for him. They escorted him to a limousine and he was driven to a big house and taken to a room where he was left alone with some bloke wearing a dressing gown who offered him a large sum of money to leave the country and never see or contact his wife again. Now, Fat Eddie knew that she was seeing someone else and was about to elope with him because he had been following her around and eavesdropping on her conversations, so he took the money and was on his way to Italy the next day to stay with his grandmother before the husband realised that he had given the money to the wrong person. With both Fat Eddie and the woman disappearing around the same time, the banker put two and two together and got the wrong answer, but a few days later the woman and her lover were found naked in a B&B in Bognor Regis when fire-fighters and paramedics were called after cries for help had been heard from inside a locked and chained door. The naked woman was handcuffed to the bedposts and her lover was lying unconscious on the floor wearing nothing but a Batman mask having hit his head on a light fitting after attempting to leap onto her from on top of a chest of drawers. The disgraced woman went back to her husband, but the incident had got into quite a few of the papers and he filed for divorce while her lover claimed that he didn't remember who she was and didn't want to have anything to do with her. Fat Eddie opened a restaurant with the money he got and is doing very well. He is afraid to go back to England in case he is hunted down for the money but says that when he's rich he'll pay the man back. I've been juggling through France and Switzerland on my way down to see Fat Eddie for the first time since the misunderstanding with the Swiss banker."

When they arrived in Milan Joe was eager to try some genuine Italian pizza before catching the next train down south, but Tom didn't want to eat near the station in case it was more expensive, so they walked around until they found a pizzeria they liked the look of, but they were quite disappointed with the pizza. Tom said that he had had much better pizza in Finland. After eating, Joe chose a spot to show Tom his juggling skills, making a bit of money in the process, and then said that he needed to get to the station to catch his train. They agreed that when they were both back in London they should meet up for a pint.

With the train to Paris not leaving until just before midnight, Tom had a lot of time to take in the sights of Milan and soak up the atmosphere, though the heat made it feel less appealing with the weight of his luggage on his back and he half-heartedly walked in the direction of a cathedral some locals had mentioned.

As Tom was walking through a park on his way to the cathedral, he heard English being spoken by a girl with blond hair wearing a short light-blue dress and a white headband, who was addressing a small boy with dark hair and glasses, so he asked her about the cathedral and if it was worth visiting. The girl said that it was very popular with tourists and was a great meeting place for natives too. She said that she liked it very much herself and offered to take him there if she could first take little Gianni home to his parents. She explained that she was Nancy from Boston Massachusetts and was working as a nanny for an American man with an Italian wife who wanted their son to be exposed to the English language.

She said, "When I replied to the ad in a magazine back home, I didn't think I stood much of a chance because I didn't speak any Italian, but that turned out to be an advantage because they wanted Gianni to have to communicate in English. His father, Harry, is often away on business and his mother, who has a strong Italian accent, never speaks English with him. When I arrived almost seven months ago, he hardly spoke any English at all, but now he is practically bilingual."

They took Gianni home to his mother and at the same time Nancy took Tom's luggage and left it in her room, making the walk to the cathedral much more pleasant for him. The cathedral was indeed grand, and Tom took quite a few pictures and as they strolled back Nancy told him how much she had enjoyed being his guide and spending time with someone close to her own age, but when they got back her demeanour suddenly changed and she became panicky saying that her employer, Harry, was back a day early.

"If he sees you with me, he could fire me. It's in my contract; I'm not allowed to fraternise with anyone of the opposite sex. I managed to get your backpack past Raffaella, but it will be much harder smuggling it back past Harry. You might have to wait until they are getting ready for bed. After that, they put the alarm on, and I will not be able to open the front door without waking everyone up."

"Why don't you say it belongs to a girl you just met?" asked Tom.

He had barely finished his question when a man's voice was heard from a window shouting, "Who are you talking to?" Without waiting for an answer, the man strode towards the front door. It was too late to do anything. Nancy stood there nervously awaiting her fate. The front door opened and a very determined-looking man came out and walked straight towards Tom saying, "You must be Tom; why don't you come in? Johnny has told me all about you." Tom followed Harry in and was introduced to Raffaella who said that she had just put Gianni to bed. Nancy was surprised and relieved at Harry's friendliness towards Tom who was also pleased to see that Nancy's fears had been unfounded.

Harry explained in his broad Texan accent, "Nancy knows that she shouldn't bring guys home, but you are an English-speaking tourist and that's good for Johnny as long as one of us is here. Of course, we don't let Nancy get friendly with local men while she is living under our roof. A couple of years ago an American student studying here met an Italian man at a nightclub and ended up with him at her apartment. He took advantage of the poor girl sexually and when she woke up in the morning he was gone, and so was her money and anything else he and his accomplice thought worth taking. A few months later she was at another nightclub when the same man, who had not recognized her, tried to chat her up. She played along with him knowing that he would ask to go back to her place. When it happened, she said that she would have to phone to make sure that her roommate would be away that night but phoned the police instead. As soon as he arrived at her apartment, he recognized it and made some excuse to leave, but it was too late; the police arrived and arrested him. You have to be very careful these days."

Harry said that he hadn't eaten and asked Tom if he would like to join him for some homemade Italian food and wine, which he said that, unlike Italians, he drank without adding water. As it started to get late, Tom mentioned that he had a train to catch, hoping that Harry would put his mind at ease by offering to give him a lift to the station. However, Harry didn't budge, and with time running out, Tom finally asked him if he would give him a lift. Harry shook his head and said, "I can't drive, I've been drinking. I don't want to end up bribing someone to get my license back."

He gave him directions and said he would just about make it on foot if he hurried, or he could take a cab. Nancy brought Tom's luggage from her room and saw him to the door where she asked him to write to her when he got back to England. Tom hurried towards the station, looking at his watch every few minutes and ended up walking the last 10 minutes like a marathon walker, hoping that he would not have any problems finding the correct platform.

The first compartments on the train were quite full, but the third compartment that he peered into was occupied by a tall girl with light brown hair wearing dark blue jeans and a light-coloured blouse. He walked in as the train began to move, sighed with a smile and mentioned that he had nearly missed the train. The girl smiled and said that she was glad he had managed to catch it. She said that her name was Gabriella and that she was from Colombia but was on her way to live in Sweden where she would be studying Swedish and then agriculture at the University of Uppsala. Tom suggested that they should make themselves comfortable for the night before other passengers joined them, and Gabriella jokingly said that they should chain and padlock the sliding door. She explained that on another overnight trip she was sharing the compartment with two Australian girls and an American guy who insisted on chaining the door so that nobody could get in, as he had met several girls who had been robbed on overnight trains in that area. Moments later a portly woman dressed in black made her way to their compartment and sat where Gabriella had intended her feet to be, but she merely bent her knees and continued to sleep. Tom opened his eyes several times during the night to find the woman sitting with her eyes wide open, but was finally relieved to see her in the same position but with her eyes closed and her faint snore being drowned out by the monotonous sound of the train chugging along the track.

Day 31 Wednesday

The woman left the train at Dijon, while Gabriella and Tom continued to sleep until it was time to take turns brushing their teeth just before arriving in Paris. Gabriella had said that she would like to have breakfast by the River Seine, and so they refrained from eating anything on the train. After Gabriella had left her suitcase in a locker at the station, they walked down to the Seine, where they took some steps down to the riverbank and sat on a bench to eat some of the food they had been carrying with them.

"What were you doing in Italy?" asked Tom.

"I went there to bury my brother," Gabriella replied joyfully with a smile that shocked Tom and left him visibly in need of an explanation.

"My brother David was two years younger than me, and we were best of friends. We were inseparable even though we had our own friends too. We knew that we could talk to each other about any kind of problems we had. Our elder brother had moved to the United States where he had a very responsible and well-paid job. David was keen to follow in his footsteps and get a good education to be able to get a good job and start a family and also support our mother financially when she got older. He never really talked about girls and was more interested in his grades, until one afternoon when he told me that he had fallen in love. I had noticed that he had been quiet and seemed a bit nervous for a couple of days but was sure that he would confide in me when he was ready. He was trembling with excitement as he told me that he had met a girl called Violeta who was the girl of his dreams with mesmerising blue eyes and beautiful hair. He told me that he had a love

218

rival and didn't know what to do. I told him that he should ask her out on a date before it was too late. His love rival was Jorge, known in the area for being rough and was the leader of a small gang that often got up to no good. He had broken the heart of several girls, while David was, in my opinion, the kind of guy any mother would like her daughter to marry. The next day David took my advice and when he returned home, I could see that he was extremely happy and excited. Violeta had agreed to go on a date with him that Saturday evening and for David time couldn't pass fast enough. Saturday evening arrived and David went off to meet Violeta, with our mother wishing him luck as if his life depended on it. I was sure they would have a great time together, but less than two hours later, he returned with a face like death. He said that soon after he had arrived for the date, a man drove up to him and asked him if he was David waiting for Violeta. When he said that he was, the man said that he was Violeta's father and as a responsible father he had to know who his daughter was dating. The man said that he wanted to have a chat with David over coffee and if he approved, he would take him to Violeta with his blessing. David was confident and so he got into the car and was driven to a coffee shop where the man told David about Violeta, her childhood and how much she meant to him. He then asked David about his family, ambitions and his intentions regarding Violeta. After David had answered all the questions, the man said "I don't have a strong opinion about you, but I think you are wasting your time because I know my daughter is in love with someone else. I am sure she only agreed to go on this one date with you to make her true love jealous. With that the man left the coffee shop, got into his car and drove off, leaving David to find his own way back to his date. As David was rushing back to the point where he was to meet

Violeta, suddenly his world collapsed in front of him when he saw Violeta through a restaurant window sitting at a table with Jorge reading a menu. Jorge was probably the only person in the world David despised and seeing the love of his life romantically involved with this person was unbearable. He put the flowers he had bought her in the nearest trash bin and walked slowly home. He told me that putting the flowers in the bin was like putting them on his own grave. David was never the same person after that. He avoided Violeta but was finding it difficult to get over her. One day he met an Italian man called Dario who was only a few years older than him but said that he already had his own business in Italy and seemed to be quite successful. He suggested that he could move to Italy and study engineering, which is what David wanted to study. He said that he knew the right people in Italy and promised to help him with the official paperwork to get a permit and a place at the university. I was already preparing to move to Sweden and as our mother is from a big family, he wasn't worried about leaving her. It wasn't long before we were at the airport seeing David off. He soon contacted us to say that he was sharing an apartment with some young people and working in the kitchen of a pizzeria in lieu of the rent and food because he was not allowed to earn money without a work permit. The last time we heard from him, things were going well. He was out of the kitchen and delivering pizza by motorbike because they were afraid that during a random inspection the authorities might ask to see his work permit. He liked delivering pizza because he could get tips which he was allowed to keep. He also said that Dario was dealing with his work permit and enrolling him for an Italian language course at the university. A couple of days later I got talking to a very nice young girl who turned out to be Violeta. When I told her that I was David's sister she said that he was sick in the head for asking her on a date and then not turning up. She said that he got pleasure from doing that kind of thing which he had done with other girls too. I was sure she was mistaken and asked for an explanation. She told me that when she arrived for the date David was not there, but standing there was Jorge who told her that David had no intention of keeping the date and was having a business meeting with a man in a coffee shop. He told her that he could prove it to her if she would agree to dine with him that evening. Violeta said that she had turned Jorge down several times because it was David she liked, but agreed to give him a chance when he showed David at the coffee shop in conversation with an older man she had never seen before. She said that she had a meal with Jorge that evening but felt very uncomfortable with him and didn't want to see him again, tough she was still very angry and disappointed with David. As I told her David's side of the story, signs of relief began to blossom on her face. After that, we did some investigation and found out that the man who had claimed to be Violeta's father was actually Jorge's uncle. I knew that David was beginning to enjoy his new life in Italy and was considering whether or not I should tell him about Violeta when we received a call from the Colombian embassy in Italy to say that he had been killed in a motorbike accident. I was devastated and immediately booked a flight to Italy. My anger towards Jorge grew to hatred but there was nothing I could do. I kept on thinking that had it not been for Jorge's deception, my brother could have been happy with Violeta instead of lying dead in an Italian morgue. I was met at the airport by a representative of the embassy who took me to identify the body. It was the most difficult and unpleasant thing I had ever done. I never thought that seeing a corpse would make me so happy, but the body of the young man lying in front of me did not belong to my brother. I stood there speechless waiting for them to show me another corpse, but that was it. That was why I had flown to Italy. There had been some sort of misunderstanding. It was like waking up from a nightmare but still being asleep. I had no idea where my brother was and why he had been reported dead. A nurse at the hospital kindly took me home and said that I could stay with her while looking for answers. I phoned my mother to tell her that David might still be alive. I knew that David had been working at a pizzeria, so I spent the next days visiting all the pizzerias I could find, asking if anyone had seen him. One day, I was near the university when I suddenly got the idea that, as he was going to study there, they might be able to help me find him. The staff were very friendly but couldn't find anything about David on their records. I felt very low but as I was leaving the university, suddenly I came face to face with David. He stood there for a second or so gaping as if he had seen a ghost, then we ran into each other's arms. I held him as tightly as I could and couldn't stop crying. He had had no idea that I was in Italy and that he had been reported dead. We immediately phoned our mother to give her the good news. I spent five days with David during which time we found out that Dario was a criminal who had no intention of applying for a work permit or a university place for my brother but intended to steal his identity. One rainy night, he was speeding home on his motorbike, when he lost control and collided with a truck. He died with the only form of identification being my brother's passport as he was trying to get rid of his own identity. Without checking properly, the hospital handed the passport over to the Colombian embassy who contacted us straight away. I don't know what role the police played in this, but the mistake caused a lot of heartache, and I think we should get compensation, though in David's opinion there is too much corruption in the Italian legal system for any justice to come out of it. When I told David about Violeta, he decided that he wanted to go back to Colombia and be with her. I was able to get the name on my flight changed so that he could use it, and I am taking the train to Sweden that will get me there a little bit sooner than I had planned but I will get to see a bit of Europe on the way."

Gabriella wanted to see the sights of Paris before embarking on her 24-hour journey to Sweden that evening and Tom, who had a few more hours than Gabriella in Paris, was eager to spend some time with Becky before heading back to London, so after breakfast Tom and Gabriella walked for some minutes together before going their separate ways. Tom was pleased with himself for remembering how to get to Becky's flat without looking at a map, and was at her front door just before noon. Not knowing her work schedule or even if she would be working that day, he rang the doorbell and began to compose a short letter in his head asking her to stay at home when she returned. He rang the doorbell again and was just about to reach for pen and paper when a neighbour appeared and asked something in French with a worried face, that Tom didn't understand, but another neighbour who was passing stopped and joined in the conversation and in broken English asked Tom,

"You want woman who live here?"

When Tom nodded "Yes," she said, "She in ospital viz ambulance."

The woman took a receipt from her shopping bag and scribbled something on it that looked like Mlle Martins and the address of a hospital. Tom thanked the women and walked away in dismay with the address in his hand until he got directions to the hospital. The hospital was a bus ride away and he was given directions to the ward at the reception desk. At the ward, he showed the piece of paper to a doctor who told him the room and bed number and said that the patient had had a dizzy spell and fallen down a flight of stairs resulting in head and facial injuries and a broken collarbone. He said that her face was badly bruised and that she had received cuts to her head and had been concussed but was recovering. When Tom walked into the room, he noticed a small family of wooden elephants and a bowl of fruit on a bedside table next to a bed bearing the number the doctor had mentioned. The bruised and battered face of the woman lying there looked nothing like the smiling face he had waved goodbye to at the station less than a month ago, and as he walked towards her, he recognised even less, until he found himself staring at a woman he had never seen before. Showing the piece of paper Tom said, "Sorry, I'm looking for Mademoiselle Martins."

"I am Mademoiselle Martins," the woman replied in a husky voice, looking at Tom in expectation. When Tom said that he was looking for Rebecca, the woman explained that she had rented her flat to Rebecca on a month-to-month basis while staying with her son and his family, but Rebecca had recently moved to a flat provided by the company where she was working. She said that she didn't know Rebecca's new address but when she got out of hospital, she could try to find it through the person who had put Rebecca in touch with her. Tom was leaving that night, so he wished the woman a speedy recovery and left the hospital relieved that Becky had not been injured, but at the same time feeling sympathy for the woman whom he hardly knew.

He walked to the Eiffel Tower where he had spent time with Becky hoping that he might see her there but knowing that it would probably not happen. There were a lot of tourists there drawn to the Eiffel Tower, as he had been on his first visit, but this time he had chosen it as a familiar place rather than as a place of interest, and he soon felt that he would rather see something new, so he left the Eiffel Tower behind him and walked until he found a place he liked and sat on the grass to finish the snacks he had been given in Liechtenstein, though there was still quite a bit of chocolate left.

Tom noticed a girl with long brown hair wearing shorts, sunning her long shapely legs, who was reading a book in French. As he was getting up to leave, the girl rose too, and as she was passing him, he asked her if she spoke English and if she knew Paris well. She said that she was originally from Bordeaux but knew everything there was to know about Paris. When he asked her what was worth seeing, she said, "I lived in America for a year with my parents and brother a few years ago and saw a lot of places there, but nothing compares to Paris. Everything in Paris is worth seeing and the nightlife is fantastic."

Tom said that he had seen most of the famous places and wanted to see something more obscure. She said that she was going to meet some friends and said that Tom could join them to see how young Parisians spent their time. She said that her name was Fabienne and that she was studying art in Paris and as they continued to walk, she went on to talk about her time in America and how it helped her discover her identity. After about 10 minutes of walking, Fabienne rang the doorbell of a flat where they were welcomed by a young man called Marc with brown hair and a fringe that was combed neatly to one side. He showed them into the living room and introduced Tom to

Marie-Pierre who struggled to speak any English at all. Marc asked if they would like some coffee and Marie-Pierre reacted to their nods and went into the kitchen returning with a fresh pot of coffee moments later. As Tom sat sipping his coffee and sampling a chocolate croissant, Marc asked him why he was there, but when he began to say that he was on his way back to England after travelling around Europe, Marc interrupted him and said, "No, I mean why are you in this world? Have you ever thought about it? What is the reason for our existence? Do we just live and die without serving any purpose? Do you believe in heaven and hell?"

Tom said that he hadn't found an answer yet, and Marc continued,

"I believe that we are all living in hell where we are condemned to death, but we can turn it into heaven by being good collectively thus finding immortality. If everyone was good, the world would be a much better place, and we wouldn't waste our time fighting each other. Instead, we would put our brains together and soon not only eradicate all diseases, but also solve all environmental problems and live forever without our bodies getting worn out."

Marc went on to talk about Philosophy with Tom while Fabienne spoke in French with Marie-Pierre until a short dark-haired man with glasses arrived, said that he was Jean-Paul and sat down for a coffee. Fabienne said that they were going to a restaurant where they would be meeting some other friends for a celebratory meal as two of their friends had just announced their engagement. She said that it would be nice if Tom could join them, adding that they would be going to a nightclub after that and that he could stay at her flat if he had nowhere to stay, but Tom said that he had a train to catch and didn't want to miss it

226

as his Interrail ticket would expire at midnight. They all left at the same time and walked a few blocks together before Tom said goodbye and turned towards the station, but the closer he got to the station the more he regretted not taking her up on her invitation and paying the extra fare to England a day or two later, but by then it was too late as he didn't know the name of the restaurant and would almost certainly be unable to find them and would miss his train too if he started to look for Fabienne and her friends.

Tom boarded the train to London with a feeling of unfinished business in Paris but also excited about the prospect of seeing his friends and family after being away for a month.

It was with mixed feelings that he took his seat where he sat quietly until an oriental-looking man excitedly asked him if the train was going to London. Soon after the train's departure, the man unwrapped some food, which he offered to Tom, but Tom recognised it as sushi, which he had tasted before, and politely declined. The man explained that he had prepared it himself at his Japanese restaurant, leaving Tom with no choice but to accept his offer and taste a bit, which he found slightly more tolerable than his previous experience. The man said that his name was Hitoshi and that he was on his way to a wedding in Oxford.

He said, "My cousin was visiting some of our relatives in England when she met an Englishman who said that he had seen her the previous year in Japan. At first, she thought he was joking, but then he mentioned the small town she was from and told her what she had been wearing that day. They hadn't spoken on that occasion, but he said that he just could not get her out of his mind and had returned to that same spot at the same time every day until it was time for him to fly back to England. He said that when he got back to England the only way to keep himself from going crazy was to convince himself that he had been hallucinating. My cousin said that although at first she was flattered, she thought he was just a weirdo with a good memory. But she allowed herself to get to know him and soon began to develop strong feelings for him. As she has some of her relatives in England plus me in France, and he has all his friends and relatives in England, that is where they chose to get married. I have been living in Paris for almost a year and this is the first time I am going to England, so it will be nice to see my relatives who live there and also those who are flying over from Japan. The wedding is on Saturday in Oxford, but my relatives will be meeting me at the station when I arrive and showing me around London for the next two days before we all go to Oxford."

Hitoshi spoke good English but had a very strong Japanese accent that took a bit of getting used to. As the train reached its final destination, Tom and Hitoshi were both excited, but for different reasons. Tom was glad to be back in London and looking forward to seeing his family and sleeping in his own bed, while Hitoshi was visibly excited to be arriving in London for the first time and as he stepped off the train he looked with anticipation for his relatives, but Tom said that they would probably not be allowed on the platform without tickets.

When Hitoshi left the platform, and did not see any relatives waiting for him, his excitement turned to worry. Tom didn't want to leave Hitoshi alone, so he waited with him for a while, looking around to see if they had perhaps gone to the wrong platform. It was becoming clear that they were not at the station, so Tom thought that they might have gone to one of the many other London stations and asked at the station office if they could contact some of the other stations to see if a group of Japanese people had gone there by mistake to meet the train from Paris.

Within ten minutes, news came that they had found Hitoshi's relatives, and not long after that they arrived at the correct station and were reunited with Hitoshi. Tom left the station while being repeatedly thanked by a bunch of Japanese men and women gently bowing in his direction and after a short wait took the local train and bus home.

It was quite late when he arrived home and quietly opened the front door so as not to disturb his parents in case they had gone to bed, but they had been expecting him and were still awake waiting for him in the living room. As soon as he saw his parents, Tom realised how much he had missed them, but he had been too busy travelling and meeting people to feel anything at the time. He also realised that he was quite hungry but luckily his mother had prepared a meal for him, which she promptly warmed up, and as he tucked into it his parents listened with interest to the pick of his European adventures until he announced that he was too tired and promised to continue at another time. After being away for a month, sleeping in his own bed gave him an extra feeling of comfort and he was soon fast asleep.

Thursday back home

Tom was already awake when his brother George put his head round the door, against his mother's instructions to let Tom sleep a bit longer. But he had slept enough and was ready to get up and start his first full day back in England. He had been lying in bed rewinding the past month in his head. His maiden voyage seemed like a lifetime ago. He was now an experienced traveller.

As he looked out of his bedroom window that he had just opened, he saw everything in a different light. The familiarity of the view and the slight smell of damp leaves that he associated with suburban London, where he had grown up, and where his parents and younger brother still lived, was comforting, but beyond his ocular vision there was a whole new world etched in his memory. He felt more confident and even excited at the prospect of socialising in multicultural London.

After breakfast, he checked his mail and was pleased to see that several of the people he had met had already written to him.

He was particularly pleased to have received correspondence from Sinikka who apologised for not meeting him at the station in Budapest. She explained that on the way to the station, her sister suddenly remembered that she had left her toiletry bag with all her makeup in the hotel bathroom and had to go back and get it, which meant that they just missed the train. She said that she was very disappointed at the time but was hoping to see Tom soon as she would probably be spending some time in England as a trainee nurse. There was also an explanation from Satu saying that she had spent that weekend in Helsinki looking for a flat closer to the university where she could be more independent but didn't want to tell her landlady until she had found a place and knew she was leaving. Her father was telling the truth about her being in Helsinki, and her landlady thought she was telling the truth too.

Later that day, Mara phoned to say that she and her mother were in London and asked if Tom would like to meet up with them. He arranged to meet them at their hotel the following day, and spent a very pleasant day showing them around London.

On Saturday while Tom's mother was preparing lunch and his father was mowing the lawn, the doorbell rang, and George went to let his grandparents in. They were pleased to see Tom and had a lot of questions about his time on the continent. After lunch, Tom and his grandfather went into the garden and sat at the same spot where he had said that he wanted to write a novel.

His grandfather asked, "Did you meet anyone who could give you an idea for a novel?"

"Well," replied Tom, "I met a lot of interesting people, but never really got round to asking them for ideas for a novel. But I know that I have been bitten by the travel bug and will meet many more people on my future travels. Hopefully, someone will give me an idea for a novel."

INDEX

www.ingramcontent.com/pod-product-compliance
Lightning Source LLC
Chambersburg PA
CBHW030139180626
46812CB00002B/761